THE ASYLUM OF APOSTLES

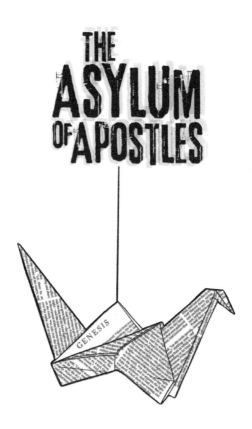

MONIQUE MÜGE

Publisher: Independent Publishing Network
Publication date: 24/07/ 2024
ISBN: 978-1-80517-757-9
Copyright © 2024 Monique Müge

For business enquiries please contact Monique Müge via email at: moniquemuge@gmail.com

Cover art created by @mogeegy

To those who fight the hard battles within us.
Every
Single
Day.

Art is, in its simplest form, the truth of God. It has no boundaries, speaks openly and without fear, but above all, is unforgiving to its creator. Just like us humans were to our creator. We knew no boundaries, no fear, and thus … here we are. Abandoned pieces of art.

- Arlo Alonso

The Asylum of Apostles

Chapter One

The Book

Have you ever been so lost in your mundane life that you've questioned why you even exist? That you have openly attempted to process why you were created and what purpose you serve the overpopulated sphere you live on? I remember thinking about it, a little too hard, that one particular evening. It already felt unsettling. The sky outside was an unnatural shade of bright pink, and I couldn't help but think about all those dystopian films that displayed such skies to indicate how screwed up the desolate world had become. I mean, think about it. Why did every disastrous film have such warm skies? Like that was meant to be some comfort to all the victims of the growing nuclear mushroom looming in front of them?

Arlo once called me cynical for saying that. That I was taking the beauty out of the wonders of nature and trading it for a depressing outlook on everything. I always found comments like that to be nothing but a contradiction from him. The big important writer who makes his millions out of drama. Not your everyday drama, may I add. None of the regular shit you see on TV all the time. No rinse and repeat. None of that hero gets the girl and let's blow stuff up crap. No. Arlo was, in his terms, a visionary, an artist! Everyone loved Arlo - everyone but me, his actual wife. I made a huge mistake marrying him in hopes that he would remain interested and invested in us. But just like a new toy, he got a few playful uses out of me and threw me to the side like I was no longer exciting. Then again, Arlo once said at a dinner party, to a full table of prestigious guests no less:

"How can I be stimulated by the same thing over and over again? As an artist, I must seek every corner of the Earth and beyond! That is where true passion lies. The need to always explore."

I then made a joke that the Earth was actually round and, therefore, had no corners for him to explore, unless you were one of those tragic flat Earth believers. You can imagine how that went. The joke fell as flat as his theory on the globe.

My hands were sore that day from folding so many pieces of paper. I had become an expert at paper manipulation, at this point, and even more of an expert at YouTube tutorials. I was making paper cranes, and since we had run out of paper, I had started tearing into one of the many books Arlo dumped around the house. But I just couldn't focus as my fingers traced the score lines of the pages in front of me. The sky outside the large, decorated window I was facing had captured me. I had to keep asking myself why I was so fussed about what was happening outside when I was in my favourite place - my room. It's not where I slept, but it was where I spent at least three quarters of my day, every single day, doing things like I am doing now, just wasting time with hobbies one would actually call art. You see, it's not that I don't think writing is an art, because I genuinely love books, and I read all of the time. I just don't like Arlo's books, which is ironic considering half of England wanted to get into bed with my husband because of said books. I mentioned he's a millionaire, right? From his writing of fiction that honestly should probably have granted him a one-way ticket into an asylum a long time ago.

There, I finally finished it. Another origami crane for the collection. My 100th one of the day, in fact. I lifted myself from my cross-legged position on the floor and got up on the stepladder to carefully hang the crane from the ceiling. Number 100 was now a part of its flock. The flock was all different, sprawled out across the ceiling in different sizes but each in the shape of a perfectly crafted crane. Every one of them was numbered individually from the pages they were conceived, like test subjects in a lab. I stepped back down to look up at my creation. A beautiful flock of displaced birds hanging in the devilish red glow of the evening. I remember looking up at them and thinking how alike we were – these gorgeous birds contained in a meaningless room and a young, bright woman drowned in the shadow of her older, successful husband.

"Mrs. Alonso? Dinner is ready."

I looked back at the maid. Yeah, we had one of those. A small woman whose wrinkles read like words in a book, stories upon stories of the hard life she lived. Her life was, no doubt, harder due to looking after the bastard, Arlo, sitting at his desk upstairs.

"Thank you, Agnes. I will go get him."

That was the marker, that awkward time of the day I had to see Arlo. I had to tolerate Arlo.

"Is there anything else I can do for you today?"

"That will be all, thank you. See you tomorrow, Agnes."

She offered a sympathetic smile, as she always did, and started removing her apron as she walked away. Agnes was set to finish her shift at the same time she always did. She always locked the immaculate house up for the night as she left too. Agnes was honestly a godsend.

Shortly after she had left, I made my way to fetch Arlo

for dinner. I really didn't want to, but the man had to eat. The house always felt barren, and as I walked through the corridors with my hands grazing the fancy wallpapered walls, without a single photo in sight, nothing to resemble a home, I compared it to a shell. Arlo and I were just crabs hidden away in this shiny, fancy shell, like pathetic hermits. The worst part about going to get Arlo for dinner was the fact I had to make my way all the way up to the loft. Have you ever had to navigate a whole mansion to get to a loft? It wasn't fun. Especially when the rest of the house was nothing interesting to explore. I always wondered why he had made his lair so far away from everything. He had so many rooms to choose from, and yet he would rather sit up in the loft to do his dark bidding. I thought devils lived below us, not above us. Yet, Arlo would argue he was more of a god rather than a devil.

As I walked closer to his slightly ajar door, I could peep the glow of his desk lamp creeping through the space between reality and his insanity. *Click, click, click. DING.* I hated that sound so much, and it grew louder with every step I took towards him. He paused as I got to the door, as if instinctively knowing I was there to ruin his peace. I hadn't even pushed the door before I heard the loud sigh he gave me. Arlo wouldn't even waste time looking back at me.

"How many times, Kate?" He paused before continuing. "How many times!"

He didn't even glance over his shoulder as he shouted at me; he just marginally tilted his head to the side so his cheek and glasses were visible.

"Dinner is ready, Arlo."

"You don't listen, do you? I don't care about dinner!" He had thrown something onto his desk in front of him, probably a pen. "I don't want dinner, Kate. I'm busy!"

"I haven't seen you at dinner in over three days, Arlo. Are you even eating? Your work isn't everything."

What the hell did I even care? Like he would worry over me? I knew I had made a mistake with what I said the minute he turned in his chair to look at me. He was triggered, and his flared nostrils and deep frown had made it obvious. The rim of his round glasses shined brightly, but his crazy, dark curls merged with the shadows like the rest of him. Just like the shadow of a man I once knew.

"It is everything …" He spoke sharply but remained calm. His eyes were wild and black, no colour left in the soul that lived behind them. "How could *you* possibly understand? I have to finish this; I am running out of time."

That "you" felt too personal. What was that supposed to mean? That I was too stupid to understand ambition because I was never allowed to have my own?

"Is it more important than your wife?" My breath was short between words. "Than us?"

It was such a stupid question. I already knew his answer. His back was turned to me once more, facing his priority.

"Every single time."

The clicking resumed as he got back to work, no longer entertaining me. "Get out and close the door."

So, I closed the door and made my way downstairs. I may have slammed it hard, though, enough to hear a few objects on his desk fall over and enough to make him growl like a grizzly bear in annoyance. Truthfully, I didn't care anymore. Honestly, some days I wished he would just get angry enough to demand a divorce; at least then I would regain some freedom. I would be penniless and alone, but free, nonetheless. Yet he never did.

That always confused me with him. He clearly hated me, but he would not let me go. Perhaps it was some kind of masochistic part of his character, like the torment made him work harder. But he wasn't always like that. When I first met Arlo, he was passionate about his work, excited about developing and starting new projects. We would talk for hours about his ideas, and he would smile and explain it all in detail over dinner. Sure, it was about work, but at least he involved me.

I'd hate to admit it, but there was even a time where Arlo was quite clearly in love, and the whole world knew it. Everyone got to see it. Be it at the film premiers he took me to, the book signings, dinner parties, literally all of it. He always took me with him, and we always looked the part too. In fact, everyone used to always say we were "attached at the hip" and "inseparable." Although that may have been right, I damn well wished it weren't the case now. How easily these unforgettable, joyous events turned into awkward, fake nights of pure inconvenience on my behalf. The worst part about any form of fame is the constant need to fake a smile. Honestly, not only does it give you the worst jaw ache in existence, but it just destroys the whole real meaning behind a smiling face. It makes you somewhat numb and robotic, then you can kiss your sincerity goodbye.

The kitchen was quiet, but never silent like some parts of the house were. Like the first floor, where my room sat on the front of the house where I could see the garden. Where you could see the ridiculously huge water fountain outside the main entrance, but also the main gates at the end of the drive. They were beautifully ornate, black bars trimmed with gold, and they displayed a huge 'A', because flexing your last name was extremely necessary. The gates were designed to keep people off the property for our safety, but they truly felt more like a way to keep me away from the outside world. Occasionally you would see people standing outside the gates hoping to catch a glimpse of Arlo, or sometimes to just even gaze at our house like royalty lived there. With the way it looked, you'd honestly think so. Never did I want a house so grand, filled with mahogany rococo furniture, rich ruby red damask wallpapers, endless halls of bookshelves and statues that looked like they could jump out at you at any second. It was all so lavish, such a show, and for what? He never left his goddamn office, and the house had nothing of real value and meaning inside of it.

I sighed for what felt like thousandth time that day as I finally dragged my heels to the stove. Admittedly, it did smell inviting, with its comforting aromas of tomato, herbs and freshly baked bread. Agnes was always an amazing cook, not because she knew how to cook all the fancy things Arlo was used to, but because she knew how to cook like a mother. I missed my mother every day, and something about Agnes reminded me I was not entirely alone in this world. Like that night, for example. A simple homemade tomato soup with chunks of warm bread felt like a reassuring hug from a woman who knew, all too well, the pain I was feeling. Agnes herself had experienced many hardships from her ex-husband before they finally separated, and when I lost my mother, the only person I had left in the world, Agnes and I grew closer. That was, of course, until Arlo started to notice we would talk and laugh for hours every day she was over, and Arlo did not like that one bit.

It wasn't even like Agnes was not working while we spoke; sometimes I even helped her work so we could talk more and enjoy a tea in the garden afterwards, surrounded by fragrant spring air that felt like a small kind of immunity for me. But no, absolutely not. Arlo did not only find this a major inconvenience for his work but also inappropriate for anyone to ever know any truth about our relationship. The control Arlo had on me even extended to whom I was allowed to talk to. I remember him clearly trying to justify it by making it about himself. He had told me:

"You have no idea how much people would pay to hear you moaning about me in the papers, Kate. How much people would pay to make *me* look bad. Why are you always so selfish? For once, can't you just think before you open your ungrateful mouth?"

And that was that. After that, Agnes was no longer allowed to talk to me about my personal life. We weren't allowed to laugh and empower one another as women. She needed her job to survive, and I refused to compromise that. Arlo had already convinced himself that a woman a few years shy of retiring was desperate to sell all our secrets to the media. She wasn't, of course, because I took the time to know her and appreciate what a wonderful human she was, unlike my paranoid husband.

I cleaned up my dish, even though there wasn't much left to clean as I had demolished my food. I always managed to polish up everything Agnes made for us, and sometimes even more later in the night. But that night, I didn't feel like eating seconds, courtesy of Arlo's shitty behaviour. Besides, there was one small loaf of bread left especially for Arlo to have with his soup. I could have eaten it (he would have never known), but the good person in me apparently still existed. I rinsed out the sink when I had finished cleaning my dishes. It always amazed me that our kitchen looked fresh out of a flat pack showroom. Of course, it was used often by Agnes, but there was never a single crumb in sight.

After dinner, I went straight up to bed. To the "master bedroom" as it was called. Master bedroom made it sound like Count Alonso himself resided in there with his velvet-lined coffin. Instead, it was quite the opposite at that time. There were holy books piled up high on his bedside table. I wished I were joking when I said there were about ten editions of the Bible stacked like a tower around the table, a whole mini-city of books forged by religious texts. An empire. And then there was my side of the bed - clean with a single book placed on the side. A rom-com actually, because I know Arlo absolutely hated those, and what better way to annoy the author in the house than by placing my insignificant read on his side of the bed. I enjoyed forcing him to swoop down to my level, down from the pedestal he so perfectly placed himself upon, just to remove my belongings from his side of the bed. Brilliant in my opinion. But a total failure at power play, of course. Such a small discomfort resulted to a mere thorn in the side of the beast of a man.

I didn't understand the new obsession he had with religion. He was never one for believing in God or any greater force for that matter. Yet suddenly he was reading every holy book in sight for his new project. I had no doubt it was a piece mocking religion and people's blind faith, questioning the very existence of man and turning it into a fantastical novel. His ambitions were probably set on making money when his berserk words were inverted into a feature film. People are stupid, honestly. They will follow any trend and consume any crap that's placed in front of them. Like greedy little pigs who will quite happily chomp down on human remains nonchalantly, absorbing nonsense (nothing more than the musings of a mad-man) and escalating fiction into hard conspiracy theory.

I never thought his work would take off like it did. In fact, I never thought he would make his millions from books. Naively, I was expecting an easy, quiet life in a small house in the countryside, surrounded by trees, maybe a couple of dogs to keep us company and – maybe even – children. Both of us would work from home as he wrote his novels that would help pay for the bills, but just about, while I looked after the house and made art to sell. We would be comfortable, not drowning in money with a grand house, but comfortable enough to live well and as a successful unit. But instead, he hit it big with his books. The idea of children dissipated. We purchased a huge house, and everything changed when the money trickled in. I tried not to think too hard about how life should have been. That only made me feel more depressed than I already was. Instead, I laid in bed at night thinking about how it could change, what miraculous event needed to occur to make my life better. There was only ever one escape route with Arlo, one that left me with money and the freedom I craved. And here I was, waiting patiently for the old stallion to kick the bucket. Heart attack? No chance. He was healthy and barely ate anything, let alone anything bad for him. Perhaps if I kept annoying him and making him shout, his blood pressure would one day creep so high he would just pop. Instead, he hung around like a helium-filled balloon, slowly deflating day by day, but not yet grazing the floor.

All of this was wishful thinking, of course. I knew that bastard was going to hang on to life as hard as he could. He had way too much to accomplish, and if the reaper came knocking, Arlo would probably smack his typewriter over his cloaked head. So, I settled down into the deep sheets of our bed with a meaningless rom-com novel until sleep took me faster than death would claim the demon upstairs.

Chapter Two

Death by Words

I woke up alone the next morning (that was nothing new), but I did manage to sleep in later than I had hoped for. It was already half past ten when I opened my eyes. I don't quite remember what time I fell asleep, but it must have been sudden, because my book was still half open on the bed. All the pages were now bent into themselves, and what was once a brand-new book looked worn and battered. I was so excited to get out of bed, I practically leapt out of it, because I was expecting more of Agnes' amazing food. It was only when I had made it downstairs that I remembered it was Sunday, and that was always her day off. When it was her day off, I often just stuck to eating something simple, like a bowl of cereal. Arlo hated that I was such a child when it came to cereal. But who would choose to eat bland bran for breakfast instead of the sugary, crunchy flakes I ate? Life was miserable enough without limiting what you ate, so why would I want to torture myself further?

Arlo spent many nights sleeping in his office. I don't know if it was because he wanted to be close to his work or as far away as he could possibly be from me. At first, I didn't think anything of it when he ordered a single bed "as a backup" for his hideout. I should have realised back then, honestly, that I clearly repulsed him enough for him to no longer share a bed with me. A husband and wife unable to share a bed. So, you could easily guess that, at that point in our relationship, anything physical was non-existent. Truthfully, I don't even think I would have allowed him to touch me. The days of longing had set sail, and the idea of him being naked in front of me just made me feel worse. But the weird thing about that morning was his food was still sitting in the kitchen exactly how it was left – untouched. That was something new. Something I never knew Arlo to do. Sure, sometimes he got so carried away with work he would come down to eat late at night, but he'd never not come down at all.

I don't know why I did what I did next. Why I cared enough about him to go up to his office with a coffee in my hand. It's odd, isn't it? How you can hate someone you love, but never stop caring about them. That no matter how many times they hurt us, we still do our best to look after them. Well, like I was saying, I went to take him a cup of coffee, and it was silent. An eerie kind of silence, like when you can hear a pin drop. I thought that was strange; he would usually be up writing again by now. That was when I felt it - my stomach's discomfort as my heart fell into it. Call it a hunch, a sixth-sense or whatever; I just knew something was wrong.

The door was left open, and I kept thinking back to the day before when he had most definitely told me to close it. I remember slamming that door shut, and yet it was wide open that morning. So, he did leave the office at some point? I knew he didn't go downstairs for food, so maybe he went to use the toilet or something? But no, as I peered into his office he was sitting at his desk, his back to me, just like he had been the night before. He was dead still. No typing, no clicking and no dinging. I felt sick already, and when the smell hit me - that metallic unnatural smell of blood – I gagged. I couldn't even see anything wrong at that point; I could only smell it.

What does anyone do in that situation? When you know something is wrong but you're not quite sure what. I keep being told I should have backed away and immediately phoned for the police or an ambulance. Instead, I went in further to turn him in his seat, my bare hands on his shoulders. Why? I had no idea he was dead! At the very worst, I assumed he had just hurt himself somehow. If I had known he was dead, do you really think I would have touched him? He was covered in blood, the jumper he was wearing had become tainted with crimson patches, and it had even managed to soak into his chair and the papers in front of him. At first, I couldn't quite figure out what had happened to him. Arlo's eyes were still open, pale and lifeless, and his mouth hung slightly open like he had tried to say something before his death. I lifted his head lightly, again with my bare hands, because clearly I was stupid and didn't watch enough murder documentaries on Netflix. That's when it became obvious. He had died from a slit throat.

Arlo was cold, and I remember, like it was yesterday, how his rigid skin felt under my bloody palms. I will never forget that. I had never seen a single dead person in my whole life, and the one I was touching was my husband, a man who had loved me, hated me, hurt me, provided for me and taken away from me. At first, I felt a bizarre sense of calm, like everything was okay and I was in control of myself. My mind had deceived me. I was not okay. As I went to scream out in horror, the realisation setting in, I felt my insides force themselves out of me. Imagine,

I clung onto my dead husband's corpse so I wouldn't fall over as I threw up, right next to his sock-covered feet. Like the scene wasn't bad enough already.

I broke down right there, on the spot. I tried to wipe my mouth on my pyjama top, but my stupid body wouldn't stop shaking. I was crying and not breathing. The panic and terror were too much for me; I just collapsed onto the floor, hyperventilating. I had no idea what to do, and all I could think about was how I had willed this into existence. With the stupid things I had thought, the stupid things I had said. This was my fault.

I'm not proud to admit it, but it took me just over half an hour to pick myself up off the floor and call the police. I would later be grilled on that, being told that I purposely wasted time in getting help for my husband. He was dead. Judging by the state of his clothes and skin colour, he had been for hours. What difference would it have made? He was beyond saving. The great Arlo Alonso was gone, and even the officers that had been sent out took their hats off when they saw his body. They bowed and shook their heads in sadness like it was the loss of the century. I mean, did anyone actually *know* him like I did? No. Maybe if they did, things would have been different. The problem was, Arlo had ties to the police force and had managed to befriend the Constable himself in the last year. Naturally, they were already on Arlo's side.

From the moment the police were involved, I knew no one cared about me. I knew no one cared about how I felt or if I was safe even. For all I knew, my husband had just been murdered, and that murderer could be anywhere, or anyone. But it wasn't that simple. God, it sounds horrible, but I really wished it were that simple, that some psycho had broken into our house and murdered him while I was asleep. All the doors were still locked from when Agnes had left the night before, not a single window was touched, and there was nothing on the outside security cameras we had. In fact, even our gate guard confirmed that no one had entered or attempted to enter our property. That left two possible scenarios. Two possible culprits. He had either killed himself, or I had slit his throat open. I knew, for certain, as soon as I opened the door for the police, covered in his blood and my own vomit, that I would be accused of killing Arlo.

It took less than half an hour for more squads of police and an ambulance to show up, and of course, media crews to start gathering at the gate. I remember watching the reports trickle in on the kitchen TV.

"Arlo Alonso, one of the greatest authors of our time, was found dead in his British countryside home. The police are treating the case as a *murder* but have no suspects at present."

"We are bringing you sad news today as esteemed author Arlo Alonso has been found *murdered*."

"Fans have already started gathering in mourning of the *murder* of the late Arlo Alonso, lighting candles and stacking copies of Alonso's books outside his home."

I didn't pay attention to that word – *murder*. They sat me in the kitchen of my own home as they removed Arlo's body and began scanning the house for evidence. I can still feel the prickling burn on my neck from their cold, accusing stares. They had already made their minds up it was me, and they were trying their best to prove it. Not once did anyone ask if I was okay, or if I needed anything. Even in death, I sat in his looming shadow. Instead, they had two officers stand by the kitchen doors to make sure I couldn't leave. The TV was, in fact, my only source of information. I was finding out what was going on inside my home from what was being broadcast outside my home. That is how fucked up the situation was. It felt like I was going to be trapped in that kitchen for the rest of my life.

But then the most unexplainable thing occurred. An officer, who wasn't in uniform, came marching into the kitchen, followed by a small posse. All eyes were on me as they surrounded me, like I was some kind of dangerous maniac. My heart stopped before the words even left his stern mouth.

"Katherine Alonso. I am placing you under arrest on suspicion of murder. Anything you say may be held …"

I closed my eyes and didn't even bother listening to the rest. What was the point? They were already placing my arms behind my back and handcuffing me, still in my pyjamas covered in blood and sick. It was done. They had made the call, and that was the last time I ever saw my home. I was stuffed into the back of a marked police car; not a black, unmarked vehicle. I didn't deserve that courtesy. So, you can just imagine the look on everyone's face as we drove out of the estate, me in handcuffs and a stained shirt. Instantly, jaws dropped and mics went back to mouths to declare I had been arrested for murdering my husband. I wasn't under suspicion. No. It was already out to the whole world that I, Katherine Alonso, was a brutal, unstable *murderer*.

Can you even believe, as they drove me down to the station, the officers in front were gossiping about me? Three key words: "jealousy," "money" and "crazy." They were discussing how mentally ill I must have been to be covered in the mess I was in, how the fact that I was no longer crying made me uncaring, and – my favourite – how I had been enjoying the attention I was finally getting as the paps followed us. None of that was true. Not a single word. I hadn't had a voice my whole life. I wasn't about to start screaming now. Even when I had done nothing wrong.

By the time we reached the station, a crowd had already gathered outside. The noise was unbearable and unreadable. Everything had become a blur and one loud mess in my head. They dragged me through the crowd, parting the people just how Moses had parted the Red Sea. I flinched from the shouting - forget the things people had started throwing at me aggressively. I lifted my head up as we were halfway through the mob, having just dodged a whole book being hurled in my direction, and that's when he caught my eye. Arlo. The way he stood still in the crowd, unmoving, observing, unlike the others. I blinked, and he was gone. But I swear I saw him, and I wasn't crazy.

I never was.

Chapter Three

A Special Place in Hell

I sat in the interrogation room for hours, sipping on nasty water from an unclean dispenser. I was eventually given a grey t-shirt and matching bottoms from an old locker. My hair still smelt disgusting, and I am pretty sure I did too. I told them what happened, repeatedly, and they just wouldn't believe me.

"I don't know what happened to Arlo; I was asleep. I saw him the night before, and then I went to bed. When I woke up, he was already dead."

That wasn't good enough. They had me go over every little detail again and again, asking me stupid questions.

"Can you explain why you had your husband's blood all over you, Mrs. Alonso?"

Yes. I had to touch him to check if he was okay.

"Did you throw up on your husband because you couldn't stomach what you did to him?"

And what was it I did to him? Nothing at all.

I went over it again and again. They had nothing on me, and I knew they were repeatedly asking me questions so I would slip up and say something they would happily use against me. I was exhausted, and I didn't want to talk anymore, yet they were forcing me to stay awake and talk after hours of poking at my confused brain. I had been through so much that day, and no one cared. Arlo's lawyer even refused to represent me or offer any advice. He was just as disgusted with me as everyone else was, which was problematic with what happened next.

The detectives were called out of the room briefly, leaving me with peace for the first time that day. It was when they returned with the biggest smirks on their lying faces that I knew I was in deep shit. They cautioned me to start telling the truth, or I was going to make things incredibly worse for myself. I had no idea what they were talking about, but I knew they had conjured up some magical way to lock me up.

"We found the murder weapon, Mrs. Alonso. It has your prints all over it."

I was shocked. Not in a guilty "I did it" kind of way, but just in pure disbelief.

"What weapon? I did not murder my husband!"

"Tell us the truth, Mrs. Alonso. You murdered your husband with the knife we found in his office. You wanted your husband dead."

"No, I didn't!"

Yes, I did. I did want him dead. I wanted my freedom, and I wanted a whole new life. But I did not kill him. They kept pressing me, trying to get me to confess to the murder, and I snapped. Just like that. Several years' worth of hurt, manipulation and accusation reached its peak. I was a glass bottle filled with sweetness no one wanted, and I had been so mistreated and shaken around so much, that I just exploded into a frothy mess. The shouts that left my mouth were primal. The way I flung the metal chair I was sitting on across the room was animal-like. I even got right up in the detective's face to growl my argument at him. I had given them exactly what they wanted: proof I was unstable. Was it worth it? Nope. I was instantly smacked face-down into the table and handcuffed again. To make my case even worse, I bit the officer's finger as he pushed my head down, and I must have bitten into it hard, because I could feel the warm blood trickle into my mouth. This time, they tossed me into a cell. I guess they were done talking.

I think I must have had a fortunate life. Privileged even. Not once had I ever been to a prison to visit anyone or been in trouble myself. Actually, I could have even boasted that I had a clean criminal record up until then. I had no idea what prison was like, and I wasn't keen on finding out either. Above all, I was innocent. That I was certain of.

The cell was disgusting. No way had anyone ever cleaned it properly. There were stains in the corners of the wall, most likely from where past detainees had purposefully pissed to spite the enforcement around them. The thin, lumpy mattress on the bed was no longer white, but several shades of coffee. I didn't even want to think what had caused it. The walls were thin, and I could hear them all talking outside amongst themselves.

"You know how crazy this bitch is? She had a whole room of paper cranes hung up."

"Paper cranes?"

"Yeah, origami cranes. You know, the Japanese art of folding paper?"

"Oh yeah. A whole room full? How many were there?"

"Hundreds! But that's nothing. She made them all from pages she tore out of a Bible."

"Who would tear up a Bible to make into paper cranes?

She really isn't right in the head."

"Tell me about it. Poor Alonso was living with a nutcase. Can you imagine being murdered by your own wife?"

Can you imagine being accused of killing your own husband? Dickhead. Yeah, I'll admit it, I won't lie. I did make those cranes from pages of an old Bible. But when we had religious scripts coming out of our earholes, thanks to Arlo, and I ran out of paper, what else was I meant to use? I never cared much for religion anyway, and I felt no regret tearing up that book. I know so many people who would have gasped and shamed me for it, but at that time, religion held zero value to me. I had to endure all their talking and all of their nonsense all evening - from the mouths of law enforcement, no less - and I had already been told that, in the morning, I would be transferred out of the station.

That bed was filthy, but it sure as hell brought me some kind of relief when I finally found the courage to lie on it. It had been the longest, worst day of my life, and I was bracing myself for what was to come. The TV shows I watched prepped me as well as they could, I suppose. No one ever prepares you for this moment, and all I knew was I was going to attend court at some point. Someone was going to decide if I was a guilty woman or not. Someone who didn't know me or anything about me was going to decide my fate, decide if I was capable of committing such a heinous crime. When I think about that now, I think about how quick humans are to incriminate someone rather than work hard to find the truth and achieve justice. In this case, no one cared for the truth, and what happened next was proof of that.

At first, I couldn't sleep. Not a single wink. My body

was drained and desperate for sleep, but my mind just wouldn't shut off. I mean, really, how could it? I was about to be put in prison for a crime I didn't commit, and the whole world hated me. But I closed my eyes and tried my best to nod off, occasionally reopening them to check my surroundings. I was still in my worst nightmare no matter how many times I had hoped I was dreaming. I thought I was dreaming when I saw him standing in front of me. It was Arlo. Alive. Or so I thought, because he looked like it and spoke like it. He was dressed like he had been the day before, in his beige cords and black jumper, but there was no blood. He was clean – pristine. As he always was.

"Hello, Kate."

I just stared at him in shock at first. There was no way he was real. I had sat with his dead body for half an hour that day, and he was most definitely dead.

He moved closer to me slowly, and for once, he wasn't frowning or shouting. He was serious. I must have lost my mind, because I spoke back to him.

"Arlo … you're dead. This isn't re-"

"But it is real, and I don't have much time. Kate, I need you to promise me something. That book I was writing. I need you to get it and finish it."

I laughed at that point. My dead husband was talking to me, and he was still making demands.

"Fuck you, Arlo."

My hands were shaking as I lifted a finger to point at him. I was upset, angry and more confused than ever. How was it possible? Obviously, it wasn't, and I was just one step closer to the loony bin.

"Kate, I know you're angry at me, and I am sorry. But please, get the book. I am begging you."

He walked so close to me I could feel his cold hand graze my cheek. That's when I freaked out and started to scream at the top of my lungs.

"Get away from me! You bastard! You fucked my whole life up!"

He was begging and pleading with me in a way I had never seen before. His hands held my arms as he shook me and shouted at me repeatedly about his book, right up until the guards came running in to tackle me to the floor and restrain me. Arlo vanished. Into thin air. I had no idea what was happening, and I had no idea what was real and what wasn't anymore. As my cheek touched the cold, dirty floor, I cried out hysterically about how Arlo was there and he wouldn't let me go. The guards exchanged a look that told me, right there and then, I had just gotten myself into bigger shit than I was already in.

The next morning, they brought a doctor in. Doctor Lucy. That was the very first time we had ever met. She was a beautiful woman, and when I heard her walking through the long corridors, with her bright red heels clanking against the grey floor, I knew she was out of place. At first, I suspected she was a lawyer of some kind. Her black hair was neatly up and away from her smooth, pale skin. Her eyes were dark, mysterious and unreadable. But there was just something about the way she carried herself that made it feel like everything gravitated towards her. That was the only time I ever saw her wearing something other than her white coat. I remember, very clearly, the black dress she wore and the black coat she draped over it. Her black leather gloves and the dark sunglasses concealing her eyes seemed a bit excessive. It was obvious we came from similar backgrounds. We had money. Well, I *had* money.

"Why is she in restraints? And why is she on the floor?"

She was talking to someone around me. I couldn't tell who. I was so tired, and the fact they had tied me up all night meant I couldn't sleep.

"I am asking you a question, detective. Why is Mrs. Alonso secured like she is about to kill everyone here?"

An officer to the right of me scoffed and hid his smirk. He clearly thought it was funny, or maybe he truly did believe I was about to kill everyone miraculously with my superpowers.

"Did I say something amusing?" She walked into the cell without a single ounce of fear. "You could be prosecuted for unfairly treating a prisoner. You know that, right?"

"Are you threatening us? This psycho nearly bit one of my officer's fingers off yesterday, and last night she started throwing herself against the wall screaming that her dead, *murdered*, husband was harassing her. You expect me to trust her?"

"Does she really look dangerous to you? Look at her! She's as quiet as a mouse. She is confused, stressed, mourning, and you're all feeding into her psychosis."

I heard a chair being pushed along the floor - that

horrible scraping sound like nails to a chalk board - and I flinched in attempt to cover my ears. Sounds like that always made me feel funny. The man rose from his seat and marched right up to Doctor Lucy. He was very round, and I hadn't seen him before. At least I think I hadn't. But, for sure, he was one angry man.

"You listen to me, lady! I am sick and tired of you protecting these people like they don't have to answer for their crimes! I don't give two shits that she was married to a famous man and touched fame herself because of it. She is a murderer! And if you truly think I am going to let you declare her insane and take her to your silly little house of freaks to protect her, you're dead wrong!"

She paused then, and I saw her face contort into a grim smile as she tucked a hand into her coat pocket to retrieve something. "I think you'll find she's already mine."

Doctor Lucy handed him a few papers and began walking away as she ordered him.

"I want her released within the hour; transportation has already been arranged."

He took one look at the paper, then at me, and threw it onto the floor, cursing. His officers were left speechless by whatever just happened. I had no idea what just went down in front of me. I had no idea what was about to happen to me or why. But it was fairly obvious I had no choice or say in the matter.

Chapter four

Lupinus Lodge

Don't you find it funny how "Lupinus" has loopy in it? I mean, listen to it. How was I meant to feel about going to a place like that? I was about to be surrounded by real crazy people, people who probably really did commit murder.

They told me when I was leaving that I was not innocent, and I was not being released from custody. That I was being transferred to a facility where I would be *safe* while they worked on their case. I was informed that I may be mentally unstable, and that may help me dodge a murder charge, but I was still under suspicion of manslaughter, and they would see to it that I would be placed behind bars.

Judging by her smirk, Doctor Lucy found it all quite amusing. She instructed two orderlies to take me outside and into the back of a car. Once I was there, she looked back at me through the metal grill that separated the back and the front passengers.

"You're going to be okay, Katherine. Lupinus Lodge is a sanctuary for people in your unique situation. You can rest now."

Could I, though? She spoke so softly to me, but I had just witnessed her owning the whole police station while giving that unsettling smirk. I said nothing; I was too tired to talk about it. The seats were comfy, and the gentle motion of the car moving made me feel like a child in my mother's arms. I fell asleep, and I couldn't even tell you for how long I slept or where we were going.

The car journey must have been a long one, because I slept deep and undisturbed, missing everything in between the station and the Lodge. When I had closed my eyes, we were surrounded by buildings, but when I reopened them, there was nothing but trees. Lupinus Lodge was once a mansion that housed a rich family, and it had been repurposed into a mental institution by none other than Doctor Lucy. Not the Doctor Lucy I knew, but her father. His mission had been to take in those who had plummeted from fame due to bizarre breakdowns. Some were, in fact, criminals, and some just randomly had a screw fall out. The point is, he had found their cases fascinating enough to study, but he was also the only one who wanted to take the fallen stars in. So, not only was it a win for him and his research, but it was also a win for the patients who had nowhere else to go, and no one else to turn to.

Her father had been a religious man. That was, apparently, why the Lodge had been named Lupinus. The flower was more commonly known as a lupin, a beautiful flower that stood like petal-covered pinecones in shades of blues, purples and pinks. The Lodge itself had loads of them outside, and I had never seen flowers like that before. But, of course, as if by sick chance, they held a biblical reference. The flowers were a symbol. Doctor Lucy had compared them to the flowers that were spoken of in the Book of James: just like picturesque flowers wither, those who are rich and famous will also fade. Ironic, right?

I remember that *my* Doctor Lucy explained this to me as we pulled up outside the bricked mansion. The grounds themselves were gorgeous, and even though a few patients were outside with nurses, there was nothing about the place that felt menacing at the time. From outside, you would have guessed it was a wonderful private hospital for those who could afford it. What I'm trying to say is, it didn't cry out "I'm an asylum" at all. We got out of the car, and she instantly released my restraints. She wasn't scared of me; that much was obvious. But that also told me she was either very confident in the hospital's security, or she knew I wouldn't try to run from the get-go.

"Katherine, this is your new home. I don't want you, at any point, to feel frightened that you are here. Take a look around you." She gestured at the grounds around us. "Do you see any armed security?"

I shook my head at her.

"That's because in order for you to trust us, we try our best to trust you. But if that trust is ever broken, I should warn you that you will be isolated. Is that clear?"

I nodded at her.

"Come, let me show you around."

Lupinus Lodge was very much an old mansion repurposed into a clinic, and it was obvious with how everything was laid out. After the front double doors was the foyer that still had its gigantic chandelier hanging above and its grand winding staircase directly opposite. Downstairs held the kitchens, the dining hall, the rec room, doctors' rooms and several classrooms. Upstairs was where we all slept in our own rooms that catered to us all individually. My room, for example, was the most basic. It was fitted with small adjustments that ensured I could not hurt myself while I was alone. The handrails were slanted so we couldn't tie anything to them and hang ourselves, the windows were sealed and guarded on the outside with bars, and the mirrors were made of plastic so we couldn't use them to cut ourselves with. I say this was basic because I later found out some had rooms that were made up of padded walls.

I was shown to the rec room first, and it was filled with people – too many people for my liking. There were only around twenty patients altogether at the Lodge, but with all the carers and nurses, it always felt crowded. This room was the place where most patients hung out between classes (yes, we had those; Doctor Lucy had stated they were to help us understand ourselves). The décor was odd. The furniture was worn and had definitely seen better days, and surrounding it all in bright shades of colour was a huge mural painted on the wall. It was a depiction of the garden of Eden. That much was obvious. There stood Adam, Eve and all the animals around them as they each took a side of a large tree filled with what looked like apples. Even a golden snake was seen wrapped around a branch and edging its tongue towards Eve's ear. As I wondered if one of the inmates had painted it, a red-headed woman traced her finger down the snake's spine as she made humming noises. They really were all nuts here.

Thankfully, I had missed lessons that day, and I was due to start the morning after. I can remember feeling like everyone had stopped what they were doing when we walked in and Doctor Lucy had briefly introduced me.

"Everyone, I would like you to meet Katherine."

"Hi, Katherine."

They all said it in time, like school kids who had been trained to do so. They were all dressed in white, specifically a t-shirts, trousers, and white plastic tags on their wrists. The nurses, on the other hand, all wore blue, a specific shade of baby blue that reminded you of a clear sky or the sea it reflected onto. Some instantly resumed what they were doing, whether that was playing chess or rocking back and forth, but some, I could tell, knew who I was and why I was there; it was so apparent in their hard stares, the way they looked through me as if trying to make a judgement of my guilt. No one got to ask me anything. Doctor Lucy made sure of that as she pulled me away to continue my tour.

"You will find most of the patients here keep to themselves. This isn't your usual establishment." She smiled at me as she spoke. "You don't talk much, do you, Katherine?"

I looked up at her. I hadn't realised it, but I had been following her with my face down and studying the floor. "Sorry, I just ... I don't know what's going on."

Doctor Lucy gave me a sympathetic look as she opened a door, the door I would know to be mine. She showed me to my room, which had my clothes neatly folded on the bed. Everything was white. Clinical. Like a blanket of everlasting snow had laid itself on the asylum.

"This is your room, Katherine."

I sat on the bed and looked around. It was all so much to take in, and I wondered how long it would be before I was behind bars in prison.

"It's Kate," I nodded and looked at her. "You can call me Kate."

She acknowledged me and leant up against my desk. I was allowed one of those, unlike some of the others. "You understand why you are here, don't you, Kate?"

I closed my eyes and sighed loudly. "Honestly? No. I don't. I'm not crazy, and I did not kill my husband."

"And I believe you. But your circumstances are not normal, and from what I heard, you have been seeing your dead husband?"

I rubbed my head. It hurt, and I just didn't want to have that conversation with her. "It's trauma. Shock. I don't know."

"Maybe so. Maybe not. But I think it's safer we find out here rather than with you locked away in prison to be blamed for a murder you didn't commit. I think you will find you're exactly where you are meant to be, at exactly the right time."

I will never forget the way she said that to me. That I was where I was supposed to be, and the timing was perfect. I hated that idea. It made me feel like my life was scripted and I had no control over it. Even worse, it felt like she knew how it was going to play out, and I didn't.

"How do you know I didn't do it?"

Her smile changed as I said that, into a smirk that edged too close to sinister. "I don't. I only know what you tell me, Kate. Therefore, I only know what you know. Eventually, I think we can both figure it out and find out exactly what is going on here."

"There is nothing going on here. My husband is dead, I got the blame, and now everyone thinks I am either a murderer or nuts. Either way, my life is fucked. This is the end."

She slanted her eyes slightly as she pushed her body from the desk to move closer. "That is where you are wrong, Kate. This is your new beginning. This is where you start."

She moved back towards the door, ready to leave. "You will see exactly how important you are. How big your role is in this book called life."

She paused at the door. "A nurse will be by soon to explain your daily schedule and take some tests. I look forward to seeing you in our sessions."

Before she left, I blurted it out. Maybe it was because I realised how fortunate I was to be there instead of prison, or maybe I was scared and wanted to be on her good side.

"Doctor Lucy?"

She glanced at me.

"Thank you."

She gently tilted her head and gave one small nod before leaving.

I didn't know if I trusted her or not, but back then, I recognised I had no choice at all. The nurse came in about 15 minutes later. By then, I was already changed into my new clothes. She tagged me that night with my own unique white band – the marker on my wrist that would identify me – and the device on my ankle that wouldn't let me leave the grounds and that would track me everywhere I went, every hour of the day. It was smart, really. It was still very much like prison; it was just dressed differently. They were nice enough that night to bring dinner up to my room. That was a one-off exception, a recognition of my hardships and the fear that I would break down in front of everyone. I don't remember eating much of it. I just poked at my boiled carrots and sipped my orange juice.

The food had got me thinking about Agnes. I wondered what she thought of me, if the police had spoken to her and if I was ever going to see her again. Would she have believed my innocence? Or would she have told the police how much I hated Alonso? Everything was so messed up. I cried into my food, drowning it in salt water. I had the sickening feeling that life would never be the same again. I reminded myself bitterly, that night, that I had asked for it. I had wanted it. I had been begging for a change, and life delivered. And as if in that moment life couldn't have made me feel any worse, he appeared to me again.

"Kate?"

I had already shaken my head and pointed my fork in his direction, tears still falling. "I don't want to talk to you. Go away."

Arlo stood at the desk, just how Doctor Lucy had hours before. In exactly the same position. "I know you don't want to see me or talk to me. You made that very clear when you slit my throat."

Can you believe he accused me of killing him?

"I didn't kill you, Arlo. I didn't do it!"

He pressed a single finger to his lips and smiled. "Keep shouting and they'll think you're going cuckoo again."

"Fuck you, Arlo."

He ignored me and began playing with the book on my desk. Ironically, it was a Bible. All of us had one. "You escaped prison, and now you are here. What is your next step? Therapy? Learning to forgive yourself? Teaching yourself how to stomach what you are?"

He was flicking through the pages when I threw a broccoli piece towards him. It bounced off his body, and that's when I started to panic. He was really there.

"How? You're dead ..."

"Death is but a gateway into the next stage of our existence, is it not?" He slammed the book shut with one hand and walked towards me. "It doesn't matter how I am here; the point is why I am. Do you remember what I said to you yesterday?"

I did, but I didn't care. "About your stupid book, and your half-arsed apology for the shit you've put me through? You're dead, and that's still the only thing you care about?"

"I am not going to apologise to you anymore, Kate. I have tried to ask you nicely, and now I am going to warn you one last time. What I was working on before I died, it will change everything, and you are now chosen to finish it."

I didn't understand what he was even talking about at the time. I had no idea what he had been working on or why it was so important to him. All I knew was how angry I was at him. For the life he had destroyed. "Why would I do anything for you? Why should I? I am here because of you, and I did nothing wrong."

He snorted at that, like I was comical to him. "Oh yeah? So, this is all my fault? I killed myself and forced you into an asylum? I made this hap-"

"Yes! You are responsible for all of this! You messed everything up, not me. We were both alive, Arlo, and you did nothing but treat me like I was the biggest mistake of your life instead of loving me like I deserved to be loved. You ruined me while you did everything to make sure you were happy. You couldn't stand to be around me, and now you're fucking dead and haunting me. What, you couldn't be around me like this when you were alive? You had to die to be present?"

"You never listened. Ever. I told you over and over again … this is bigger than both of us. I was-" He stopped abruptly and sighed. "I don't expect you to get this, okay? I didn't at first either. I just need you to do this. One way or another, that book must be finished."

"No, it doesn't, and I am not listening to you."

I covered my ears and began to chant loudly, "You are not here, you are not here, you are not here …"

He grabbed my wrists to try and pry my hands from my ears. Arlo was talking, but I only heard his muffled words. He had become restless, and I had become more persistent. And just like that, he was gone. I didn't sleep much that night. Instead, I sat up in bed and waited for him to return. He never did. I had no idea why I was seeing him, but I had started to consider that maybe Doctor Lucy was right. Maybe there was a truth inside of me to uncover, and maybe there was something wrong with my head.

Chapter Five
Saint Barty the Behemoth

Barty was the weirdest of the bunch. The first day I met him, I knew he was going to be trouble. Apparently, he had already been quite the handful before I got to the Lodge, but my arrival had animated him even more. I got blamed for a lot of the patients *changing* during my time at the Lodge. The thing is, I never did anything to make them change. Just like everyone else, I was trying to get on with my life quietly, and it seemed like wherever I went, chaos followed.

It was after breakfast it all started. Once again with my plastic cutlery and airplane food. I picked at it and barely ate. The food itself wasn't great, but honestly, I still hadn't regained my appetite. I assumed, at that point, they would only tolerate my poor eating habits a little longer before they'd start forcing it down my throat. Thankfully, it never got to that point. Their scary frowns and the way they would hyper-analyse me over dinner was enough to get me to eat. I was terrified of what they would do to us if we misbehaved, which was an odd feeling to have since I hadn't been threatened or seen anyone get treated badly. Something in my gut just told me to behave, or else.

Well, that mid-morning session was class drawing time. Yeah, you heard that right. Sounds silly, doesn't it? A group of adult rejects, who were once rich and famous, sitting at tables with coloured crayons to draw pictures in an asylum. We weren't allowed to use pens or pencils, just in case one of us decided to stab our tablemates. That seemed absurd to me at the time, but as time went on, I understood exactly why small precautions like that were taken. Some of their minds were just ... *different.* I wouldn't put it past a few of them to take pens apart to their smallest detail and build some new kind of contraption to take down the whole asylum. You see, there is crazy and there is genius, and they aren't so far apart.

Take Summer, for example. We never spoke much, and neither did she, to anyone for that matter. She was one of those super-quiet but deadly ones. You would always spot her out of the corner of your eye because her hair was so naturally bright. Fluorescent orange, and it was all natural; she had been in there long enough to prove it. Barty told me she once was an illustrator, and she was very good at it. Every drawing session we had, she would just zone out and create these masterpieces out of children's crayons. It was insane. Well, it turns out, so was she. Because one afternoon she threw herself off the dining room table and started drawing on the floor with food. Not just her food either! That seems tame enough, right? Wrong. She then decided to start whacking staff members on the head with the dinner trays because the peas weren't the right shade of green. Can you imagine if our forks were metal?

When I witnessed Summer do that, my first thought was how crazy she was, and how unnatural behaviour like that was. But looking back now, I see exactly why she did it. Imagine, being so good at something like drawing, and you have no way of getting it out. Her brain must have been bursting with ideas she had no way of executing. You can't put creativity in a box;

it just doesn't work. It's either going to tear the box open and leak onto everything else in your life, or it's just going to explode and make a mess. With her, I'm sure she finally exploded and attempted to break her creative restraints.

But back to my story, and enough about Summer. After breakfast, I went to drawing class, and Doctor Lucy caught me trying to sit at a table with Summer. I chose her because she was so quiet and fixated on her drawing, I was sure to have an easy two hours ahead. But, no, the doctor had other ideas for me and told me to sit at a table that already had two men sitting at it. I recognised one of them straight away, and I almost wanted to beg Doctor Lucy not to sit me there. As crazy as crazy goes, this guy was the king of crazy, and I didn't want to sit next to him. It was too late, and I soon found myself sitting between the two men at the table.

Another thing to note: the tables at the Lodge were round. Every single second felt like circle time at school. In fact, that's exactly what being at the Lodge felt like – school. You would get spoken to softly and merited like star of the week for good behaviour, and you'd often see people fight like it was a playground. So, I remember the three of us sitting around this circular table like a triangle, with exactly the same space between all of us and no corners for us to smack our heads on. There was no escape.

The idea of the class was for us to unwind, release our emotions onto paper and socialise calmly with one another. In other words, group therapy with coloured wax sticks. To the left of me sat a man I knew to be called Steven Hendrix, former lead singer of a heavy metal band called Burn the Blazers. His stage name was Barty the Behemoth. Their music wasn't actually that bad, and from what I knew, they were fairly successful. But "Barty" had had an accident on stage. It was all over the news, some kind of technical fuck up. One of the metal frames from the set had come loose during all their jumping and moshing and, thankfully, it didn't fall directly on him, as that would have killed him. It instead swung precisely and only managed to hit him. It was said the hit to his head was so hard he forgot who he was, but that's only half the story.

Barty was now, in fact, nothing like his former self. His shaggy black hair was gone, he no longer wore any dark stage make up around his piercing blue eyes, and he never even swore once. There was no rockstar left, only God. He had grown his hair out into its natural brown locks and walked around preaching the Bible. He and my husband would have been best buddies, I'm sure of it. He was convinced not only was the Bible the only truth in the world, but that he was Jesus reincarnate. Yep, you heard that right. Barty the Behemoth, former rebellious heavy metallist who hated God, was now convinced he was the next Jesus Christ and only wanted to be called Steven. Why? Because he didn't want a reminder of his burdens, or his past lifestyle. He wanted to be clean and ready for the End Day. Which, by the way, he fully believed was coming.

"Mrs. Alonso, what a privilege to have you here."

I looked up from my seat to see Barty was talking to me, his hands neatly pressed together on the table. The other guy was looking up at the ceiling but listening.

"Please don't call me that. Call me Kate."

Barty stared for a while, as if calculating what he would say next. Maybe he was waiting for God to whisper it in his ear? Either way, it pissed me off. Why was it so hard to just say what you were thinking? Not everything had to be perfect.

"Kate? Okay. We will call you Kate." He motioned with his hand. "This is Michael, and I am Steven."

I laughed at that and picked up a crayon to play with. It was blue. That over-the-top blue that didn't exist outside in the real world, only in man-made plastics.

"I know who you are. You are Barty the Behemoth."

He sighed so slowly and closed his eyes. Not angrily, but in a display of his dismay. "Please, I do not wish to be called that terrible name anymore. God has removed me from that life, and I am here to start anew."

The other guy's bushy eyebrows raised, but his eyes did not move. He looked tired and so done with all of it. I wondered how many times he was forced to sit next to Barty and put up with his ramblings. Poor guy.

I just nodded and began to scribble on the paper in front of me. Making friends wasn't really on my agenda, and I most certainly didn't want to mingle with the insane. Barty, however, can be pushy.

"What happened to your husband, I am sorry for your loss." He had edged himself towards me. "Did you do it?"

The guy next to him even gulped when he asked the question. The sheer confidence in him threw me. Who outright asks something like that?

"What? How do you even know about that?"

Barty frowned in confusion and then placed a hand on mine sympathetically. "Child, it was all over the news a few days ago. We all saw it during rec room time."

I moved my hand from his. Not only did I not want to be touched, but there was something strange about his energy.

"No, I did not murder my husband."

I must have said it a little too loudly, because the whispered conversations in the room died, and everyone glanced over at me. Doctor Lucy was slowly making her way to each table when she noticed the sudden shift in the room, so she put everyone back on track.

"Let's all focus on our drawings. Come on, I am seeing some wonderful art already."

I put the crayon down and wiped my face. I really didn't want to be there, and this was making it worse. So, I asked him something back. "Why are you here then, Barty? Because you took a big knock to the head?"

He nodded instantly. "Yes. It was about a year ago now …"

The guy to my right sighed, put his head down and found a crayon to fiddle with. He must have heard the story too many times to tolerate it again.

"I was on stage, one of the biggest shows of our tour. And by some divine intervention, BAM!" He hit the table and started laughing. "God hit me so hard. I knew right away. All the wrongs of my life and what I must do. There is so much work to be done, Kate. And I believe your innocence, but I do believe you are here for a reason. God makes no mistakes, be sure of that."

I was at a loss for words. God makes no mistakes? Then why was I in an asylum for a murder I didn't commit and seeing my dead, bastard of a husband's ghost?

"Is this yellow?"

A new voice entered the conversation, and the guy sitting next to Barty held a crayon up. It was red, and he had played with it so much the waxy residue had started to change the colour of his fingertips. Barty was still talking about his life mission and quoting scripture when I answered the man Barty had called Michael.

"Erm, no. It's red?"

I looked at him, and his eyes were ever still. They would never change. It always looked like he was staring into thin air.

"Oh. I thought I had it that time." He scratched his bearded cheek, and his dark hair stuck up all over the place as he placed the crayon back on the table. He picked up another. "Is this one yellow?"

It was green.

And I was done with this bullshit.

"Can you not see them? Are you colour-blind?"

He shook his head gently. He was timid and almost shy, which was even more odd when I later found out he was once an actor. "I can't see. I'm blind."

I suddenly felt guilty for thinking he was stupid sixty seconds ago and began to search the table for a yellow crayon. That's when I heard a snort like a pig and a shout come from the table next to us.

"No, he's not! He just pretends he's blind."

The guy at the other table had eyes as wide as one of those nocturnal animals you'd see in a jungle, and his bright, white, patchy hair wasn't helping his case either.

I was just about to say something when Barty became animated.

"He is blind! By the will of God himself! Michael had to be stripped of his vision so he could see the bigger picture! The end of the world is coming, and only those who see God will be welcome into his home. The eternal land of …"

I leant over the table to place the yellow crayon into Michael's open hand, ignoring Barty the bonkers. "It's yellow."

He smiled warmly and nodded, now trying to find his paper. "Thank you, Kate."

I sat back and watched him attempt to draw a picture with his sought-after yellow crayon. The wonkiest yellow circle I had ever seen emerged on his white paper. Barty continued screaming until Doctor Lucy got two orderlies to take him out of class to cool down. Funny, how he always spoke so calmly when they grabbed him and threatened to restrain him. He began to speak like any other sane person would. In fact, better than most. It was obvious he was highly educated, and his rockstar lifestyle had been his way of rebelling against his upbringing. Maybe he failed at his first career choice? Maybe he hated it so much he just had to do something drastic and make people's jaws drop? But the one reason people often left out when they judged people like us: maybe he just loved music, and that's what *he* wanted to do with his life.

Michael had drawn his best attempt at a sun with his tongue slightly poking from the side of his lips. For someone who couldn't see, it wasn't half bad, honestly. I began to wonder what had happened to him and how he ended up here. Was he, too, wrongfully sentenced here? My thoughts were cut short when Doctor Lucy crouched beside me.

"Hey, Kate. I'm sorry, you'll have to excuse Barty. Sometimes he can get a little excited, and I'm sure he was just happy to meet you." She smiled and looked at my paper. "What have you been drawing today?"

The page was embarrassingly covered in blue squiggles.

"I …"

She nodded in understanding.

"I know this has been hard for you, and you must feel so confused and jumbled up. A little like your drawing. But why blue?"

Why blue? Was it the first crayon I had picked up, or did I think about what colour I chose?

"Is it perhaps we are feeling a little blue? A little low in mood?"

I looked up from my page and back over to Michael's. He had drawn a bright sun bursting with rays, and here I was drawing a blue mess.

"Sometimes, after we make drawings like this, the best thing we can do is …" She took my drawing, crumpled it up and threw it to the floor. "Start again."

She smiled and placed a new piece of paper in front of me. Doctor Lucy had moved on over to talk to Michael when I began to think about what to draw next. Instinctively, I ignored the wide range of coloured crayons staring at me and began folding and tearing the paper to size, creasing it and teasing it, until I had a perfectly-made origami crane. My crane, now white and not colourful or covered in words like they used to be. Just plain, boring white. Like everything else around me.

When Doctor Lucy had left for another table, I handed the crane to Michael. He didn't care for how bland it was, how lifeless it was. To him, it was colourless from the start and still a beautiful creation. He played with it in his hands as he smiled, touching the sharp edges and flapping it gently like a bird does its wings.

"It's a bird."

I didn't smile, nor did I frown. I just watched as he played with it, flying it around him like this was the most fun he had had in a very long time. The doctor had asked me to draw how I felt, and I still longed to be nothing but a bird who was free to go wherever she wanted. But this bird was clothed in white and caged.

She was crazy.

Chapter Six

A Blind Truth

The days went by more quickly than I had expected. Day after day, pill after pill, class after class, I started to feel different. That morning, I sat with Michael at breakfast, as I had done for the past few days. There was something about him that seemed so … normal. If I had to say any one of us was wrongfully put in the Lodge, it was him. Sure, he became drastically blind, and I had learnt that was up for debate, but he was quiet, and he never pried. I had so many people that week come up to me and ask me if I had killed Arlo. Some were even staff members. One morning, I was taking my pills, and one looked me in the eyes as he handed me my little paper cup.

"Did you do it, Kate? Did you kill him?"

I was dazed by the question. Firstly, I thought they weren't allowed to ask us things like that? Secondly, he asked right out in the open, with no remorse, in front of all the others. They all waited, as if expecting me to say, "Yes, I did do it!"

Another one of the nurses had even told me that her favourite book was *Rats Among Mice*, one of Arlo's books that I always found nothing short of depressing. It was about a war that had essentially ended the world as we knew it and compared humans to rodents. The difference was some people were like mice, who were timid and stupid enough to take bait; and some were like rats, bigger beings that worked in the darkness and bided their time. It became a hit film about six years back, and since then, everyone has been reading it. Most of Arlo's work was depressing, in my opinion. When someone told me he was their favourite author, I queried if they liked feeling low and enjoyed consuming negativity by choice. There were so many books in the world that were full of love, joy and peace, but no, they wanted to read novels about disaster and hate.

I had spoken to Michael over breakfast about it, and what he said stuck with me. "It's like the Bible. It's a book, right? But it does different things to different people and makes people act in different ways. To some, it can be a relic of positivity and change; it can even save someone's life. But to others, it can be the crux of destruction; it can fuel wars and make people sick with belief. I don't think it's the book that's the problem, Kate. It's what people actually take from the words in front of them. Look at Barty, for example. Some would argue that his obsession with God has benefitted him, as he is no longer taking drugs and drinking all the time; but some may say it's made him worse, and he is now so far gone he can't come back. It's a matter of opinion and perspective, right?"

It was, indeed, a matter of perspective. Like any of us who sat eating in the hall that morning, an outsider would have seen us all the same. All dressed in matching white overalls. All of us obediently eating. All of us insane. Yet, if anyone knew a single one of us, they would have seen us for what we truly were: a room full of humans with tragic stories.

"Do you think Barty's obsession is good or bad?" I asked Michael, as I valued his opinion.

"I don't think it's for any of us to decide. Except Barty."

He smiled, and my thoughts went back to Arlo. His obsession with holy scriptures had driven him almost wild. I had judged him harshly for that, and Michael was the first person who made me question if I had the right to do so. Michael had heard whispers throughout the week that I was a murderer, and he still chose to sit next to me every day and treated me no differently.

Barty interrupted my thoughts as he sat opposite us both with his big grin. "Morning! Isn't the world so wonderful, even though it's weeks away from destruction?"

I slanted my eyes as Michael continued eating his eggs. "Morning, Barty. You know you need to stop scaring people with that end of the world stuff, right?"

Michael nodded in agreement.

"It is Steven, not Barty. But it's coming, Kate. Even your husband knew it. Better start praying, lady!"

He hysterically jumped up from his seat and began walking around the room, both arms in the air as he began preaching. I watched him weave in and out of tables as he shouted. I am sure if Jesus did exist, he wouldn't have acted that way. This was something straight from the theatre.

"Are you sure we can't judge his obsession?"

Michael laughed at that and shook his head.

After breakfast, we had the strangest class. It was my first Sunday at the Lodge, and I didn't know reading class was a thing. I half expected them to sit us in a carpeted room and make us read a book each on the floor. But that's not what it was at all. We took that class in the rec room where all the sofas were, and everyone got comfy for two hours as a book was read out loud by a nurse. Michael loved it more than anyone else. He sat on the rug cross-legged and listened with a big smile on his face. I guess it was because he couldn't read any books himself anymore. That was an assumption though, and a poor one on my behalf. Of course, blind people could read. I just meant that he hadn't been able to read anything from the very basic books that were available in the Lodge, as none of them were in braille. So, I guess reading time was the Lodge's cheap shot at being inclusive. And let's be real, most institutions were nowhere near as inclusive as they should be.

Summer was allowed to sit and draw as she listened, and Barty would occasionally nod in approval or counter that the words being spoken were not biblically accurate. But my favourite was Ella, who, no matter what class or occasion, would rock back and forth on the spot, repeatedly chanting, "Nope, nope, nope." I shouldn't laugh, but it was funny that after the end of every sentence, you could quietly hear her saying nope to everything she had just heard.

I was sitting next to the large window that day. It was the only way we could see outside, as all the other windows were smaller and frosted. This one, however, reminded me of the old window in my art room, where I could see the gate to the mansion. This gate was different. There was no shiny 'A' on it, and this one was silver, not black. The garden outside was much nicer too, maintained with fresh grass and several flower beds. I hadn't been outside yet, but I had heard that some patients liked getting fresh air with a staff member. Of course, we were never fully allowed to be left unattended, just in case one of us decided to go on an all-out rampage or prison break.

I closed my eyes as I rested my head against the safety

bars of the window. The cold metal felt more real than ever. The nurse was reading from the third chapter of *Moby-Dick,* and I wasn't listening to the words; I was just letting myself slip into relaxation amid the mumbled sentences as she droned on. That was when we all heard Michael scream out in horror.

The sounds of his screams were unnerving, and the way he was backing himself into the wall directly behind him – like he was trapped – was even scarier. He was staring towards the door as we all looked at him in disbelief. His eyes were fixated on something. A blind man, staring at something that wasn't there. Everyone was confused. Everyone but me. I saw what he was screaming about. There stood Arlo, glaring deep into Michael's soul as he screamed repeatedly, becoming breathless.

The nurses ran to Michael's side, and they tried to calm him, but he was beyond reasoning. His eyes wouldn't leave Arlo, and he started talking loudly as he threw his arms around violently.

"His throat. It's cut. He's dying!"

My heart worked its way up my throat and threatened to jump out onto the floor. As they dragged Michael out of the room – it took four of them to do it – Arlo stepped aside to make way and turned his attention to me. He waited for me to react, to say something to him, but I refused.

Michael's cries could be heard as they dragged him down the corridors, until there was silence. I knew they had injected him to hush his shouting. Everyone started whispering amongst themselves as I frowned at Arlo. It was enough he was haunting me, but now others as well? How did Michael even see him? He was supposed to be blind.

"Okay, everyone, that's enough. Let's get back to

reading time, okay?"

I didn't want to get back to reading time.

I wanted to kill the Arlo smiling at me.

That evening, I had my weekly session with Doctor Lucy. We were supposed to have these weekly one-to-one sessions to discuss our progress and our concerns, get into our heads, that sort of thing. I didn't care much for therapy, but Doctor Lucy had an interesting way with words.

"You seem troubled, Kate. Is everything okay?"

I was playing with the fabric on the seat I was sat in, the red velvet-like texture moved back and forth between my fingers. "Is Michael okay? I've never seen him freak out like that before."

Doctor Lucy gave me a small, sympathetic look and placed her hands atop her paper pad. "Michael is in isolation for now. Unfortunately, this is not the first time we have seen him break down like this. That's how we ended up taking him in. But yes, your friend is okay, Kate. Shall we start our session?"

I nodded, taking the hint she didn't want to discuss it anymore.

"How has your first week been? Any thoughts that you would like to discuss with me?"

"Am I going to prison? Every person this week has called me a murderer to my face. It's like everyone has already made their minds up."

"You told me you didn't do it, Kate. Remember when we first met?"

"Yes, and I didn't do it. But everyone is saying I did, and words hold power. So do accusations."

She nodded gently and wrote something on her paper, listening to everything I was telling her. "Let's talk about that word. Power. What does it mean to you?"

She would often ask me questions like that. Weird psychiatrist-like questions that would make your brain work too much. She had a gift for getting people to talk.

"Well, I guess it means to be able to control someone or something, to have authority over someone or something."

"Interesting. So, when we look at your understanding of power, would you say you have had power in your lifetime?"

Power? When and how could I have had any form of power? I wasn't even allowed to make a single decision, and I was constantly told what I was, and wasn't, allowed to do.

"No. I don't think so."

She nodded once more, not saying anything for a while. That often made me nervous, and I would start trying to unpick her brain with my eyes. It never worked.

"Power is all around us, isn't it, Kate?" I didn't answer her, and she continued. "If we really consider what power means, it originates from the Bible. God was described as omnipotent, to have unlimited power. But in the modern world, power might look a little different, mightn't it?"

I listened to her as I thought about it, thinking about how power had always been used against me, and never for my betterment.

"Power typically can be seen in people who rule over others and control them, right? But what if power didn't just belong to a person, Kate? There are other things in this world that can rule and control a population. Can you think of an example?"

"Faith … religion. Like Barty. His faith holds enough power to change his mindset, to change his behaviour and control him."

"Very good, Kate. So now we recognise that power can come from people, ideology … anything else?"

I shook my head at her question, not quite knowing where she was going with this.

"How about money? Is money power?"

"Money? I mean, I guess money can buy you power?"

"Yes, maybe. But what about the things people are willing to do for money? Therefore, doesn't money control people? Have power over people?"

Money was a taboo subject. Not only was money a very private and sensitive subject, but for people like all of us here at the Lodge, we had never once had to worry about it. We had always had money; we were born with it, lived with it, and we would all die without it. If money really was so powerful, then how did we end up here?

"It is considered a sin to be greedy, to crave fame and to want power. But do you think everyone with power is evil, Kate?"

"You just said God is described as 'all-powerful,' and you're asking me if everyone with power is evil?"

She leaned closer, displaying her devilish grin. "Yes."

I thought about it and snorted at the question.

Whatever answer I chose would have been wrong. If I had said yes, I was disrespectful and a non-believer. If I had said no, then I would have been a liar too.

"I think people with power, no matter who they are, can't possibly please everyone. No matter what, your power is going to offend someone, uplift someone, hurt someone and save someone. Power is subjective, and power can die just as easily as it can be reborn. Power is both liberating, and evil. There is no in between."

Her smile grew wider, and she leaned back slowly, readjusting her glasses on her nose. "If power can make both heroes and villains, what would you say you are?"

I laughed and sat up in my seat. Out of all the questions she asked me that night, this was the easiest to answer. I knew exactly who I thought I was, and I knew exactly who everyone else thought I was too. But above all, I had started to realise what I was to Arlo.

"Both."

Chapter Seven

The Good Word

What Doctor Lucy said played in my head all night long. I barely slept. I couldn't figure out who I was angrier at – her or myself? The thing is, this went on for a few days, me just being mad at the situation. I didn't like that she managed to wiggle herself into my brain like a worm and look around into my thoughts and feelings. They were mine and none of her business. I also didn't like that she had somehow made me question exactly what power I had. She was strung up on discussing power, and it made me consider exactly what she wanted the outcome of that conversation to be. So, she wanted me to be mad at my husband for taking my power away? Did she want me to be mad at myself for never having the power to do anything about my life? Or was she just screwing with my head, making me believe that power was out of our control? Either way, it triggered me.

All this God talk was getting to me even more, though. Every single day, it was mentioned somehow. I got it, I mean with the Lodge having been developed on a religious ideology and all, but it was just as bad as being at home. Sure, there were no mountains of holy scripture here like back home. Instead, there was a Bible in all of our rooms, the nurses always remind us to smile and feel grateful that God himself had given us a second chance, and I got to listen to Barty all the time. Did I happen to mention I was blessed with being on the same floor as Barty? We were practically neighbours, and he would never shut up. Some nights, he would even start singing hymns from his room. Let me tell you now, it's one thing to sing heavy metal, but to take that voice and start singing about Jesus is a whole other thing. It was the perfect assumption of dissociative identity disorder, changing from one person to another without any warning.

It was exactly three days after I had spoken with Doctor Lucy. There was no sign of Michael, and I had kept to myself as best as I could. Barty had been trying to talk to me since the incident, and I tried my best to brush him off or just ignore him. That morning, however, he was far too animated for my liking. We were in the rec room, all of us but Michael, and we usually all did our own thing. Music was playing in the background. I think it was *Satie*. I recognised it vaguely from when Arlo would listen to music as he cooked up his new schemes. I was sat at a table alone by the window as the sun warmed my skin, minding my own business with a puzzle. I am so sure some of the pieces were missing from that puzzle box. The picture was as generic as they came, a painted landscape of a flowered field with a token windmill standing amongst the cotton, clouded sky. It didn't matter what the image was; I just wanted to finish it and accomplish something for the first time since I got there.

The song changed. *Barber*. One of my favourites of his. As the strings delicately played, my insides began to flutter as if the notes themselves stroked my soul. That was the first moment after Arlo's death that I had felt weightless – listening to a beautiful piece of music through shitty tin speakers. The real juxtaposition of life and its beauty shown through tragedy.

My escape lasted all but a minute. A hot hand touched my forehead, and before I opened my eyes, I knew it could only be one person – Barty. The weightless feeling fell through me like an anchor and pinned me back to reality with a lunatic that assumed himself the next Christ.

"Child, music is that of the angels. That feeling that flows through you is a praise to God himself." His eyes were closed as he spoke, as if channelling energy from me like a battery.

He moved his hand from me and smiled warmly. "You have no idea how special you are, do you?"

I had no idea what he meant by that. He didn't know me well enough to make a statement like that.

"You don't know me, Barty. Or anything about me for that matter."

"Oh, but I do, and I know about your husband, Arlo, also." He linked his hands in front of his stomach. "Your husband was chosen to write a very important scripture. He never got to finish. Am I correct?"

There was something about the way he spoke that sent a chill down my spine that day. As animated as he had been all day, dancing and shouting around the tables, he was no longer like that at all. He was calm, collected, and he spoke with a sanity that was cutting through me like a hot knife. I was speechless as he continued.

"Michael saw him, didn't he? You saw him too."

My eyes moved over to a nurse nearby. Maybe I was considering asking for help, but for what exactly? Was I running from Barty and his madness? Or was it that I was scared he was speaking the truth and had called me out? There was no way he could have possibly known about that. No one else saw Arlo but me. And, I guess, Michael.

"Are you scared by the truth I speak, Kate?" He was smiling as he spoke, as if he were aware of where my thoughts were. My gaze must have been a dead giveaway.

"No. Because it's not true. You're just a crazy man."

"Am I crazy? Are you crazy?" He moved a little closer and whispered, "Maybe, we're both crazy?"

I shot him a warning stare. "I'm not crazy."

He nodded and scoffed in almost laughter. His counter was solid. "So, does that make Michael crazy? He saw your husband too. I mean, if you're not crazy, I'm not crazy … "

"I don't know what Michael saw, Barty. It's none of my business. He's sick, and so are you."

"We're all sick. We're all dying. This is the world we now live in. Centuries away from the perfect paradise created by God and a fresh hell created by man, no less. But being sick and insane are two different things, aren't they, Kate? Sickness is that which weakens the body, and if you ask me, insanity seems to be the new label for an open, healthy mind. So, tell me, Kate. Are you sick or insane?"

I hated the way he was talking, yet some of it made perfect sense. The previous conversation with Doctor Lucy about power brewed in my mind as he spoke. Was "insanity" in this Lodge another way of saying a dangerous, powerful mind? I mean, think about it. What if he actually was what he said he was? A reincarnation of Jesus Christ. Even when Jesus walked the earth, he wasn't accepted and was nailed to a cross. Why would Barty's treatment be any different? His words had started making my own sanity slip, and I did not like that one bit.

"Barty, I am not interested in your little mind fuck games. Leave me alone."

He refused to move and continued to speak. "Arlo won't leave you alone until you do what he asks. It is vital you do the job you were chosen to do, Kate. You are vital to God's plan."

I stood up from my seat and attempted to end the conversation. "We're done here, Barty. I have nothing more to sa-"

Just like that, Arlo stepped from behind Barty to join his cause. It was almost as if Barty knew he was there, because he began to motion a cross with his hand to his torso.

"Arlo knew the value of his mission. That mission is now yours and no one else's. You are the chosen one, Kate."

Arlo stared at me as Barty spoke. He supported him, and I truly began to wonder if I had become like the crazies around me.

"Get out of my head!" I slid the half-made puzzle across the table and towards Arlo.

Naturally, that caught everyone's attention, including the on-duty nurses. Barty fell silent, a strategic retreat. One of the nurses called out to me.

"Kate, is everything okay?"

I was not okay. Far from it, in fact. I had begun to hyperventilate and was staring at Arlo, who looked like nothing but empty space to everyone else in the room. It was then I backed away and screamed.

"LEAVE ME ALONE!"

Barty watched me as the nurses ran past him. It felt as if time itself had slowed to a halt as the light from the window sent rays around him. His right hand floated in the air next to his flowing hair, while his left hand graced his heart. The nurses were nothing but shadowed fiends around him as they ran towards me. My breath caught in my throat as his eyes met mine, and a sudden overwhelming power pulsed through me. The room started to darken around his light, and before I could speak, everything turned black.

When I awoke, I was no longer in the same place. The room was pure white – no windows and no furniture. The walls were padded with soft insulation, and the rectangular lights above me were so bright it felt like they penetrated my eyeballs. My head hurt, and I wondered if it was the lights or if I had hit my head when I passed out. I had no idea why I passed out or if anything I experienced before that had actually happened. Honestly? I didn't want to know anymore. I just wanted it all to end. But as much as I wanted that, I knew that was never going to happen. My point was proven as I heard her voice from the doorway. It was Doctor Lucy.

"Kate. You're awake. How are you feeling?"

I squinted hard at the blinding light above my head and began to move to face her. I failed. My arms were bound in a jacket, and I couldn't move my body the way I wanted to. They had put me in a straitjacket and set me inside of a padded room like I was some serial killer in a horror film. The worst part is, I was so done with everything at that point I began to laugh like said serial killer from said horror film.

"The jacket was just a precaution; we had no idea if you were going to become violent after your episode earlier." She happily sat herself on the floor opposite from me, in her white coat as always. Everything was bloody white there.

"Barty started it, not me."

"Is that so? He says you saw your husband again and became a little ... animated, shall we say? Is that true?"

Jesus complex or not, Barty was a snitch is what he was. He had calmly explained to Doctor Lucy that I had broke down about seeing my husband's ghost. Can you believe that? In no way, shape or form did he mention anything about what he said or what he provoked. Nope. He was innocent in all of this.

"Did he now? You know what? I am so sick and tired of all this bullshit! Everywhere around me, all the time. First Arlo, who is *dead*, begs me to finish this book; then Michael, who is *blind*, sees him; then even Barty, who thinks he is *Jesus*, knows about him too! I am not crazy, Doctor Lucy. I swear I'm not! But everyone is making me feel crazy."

She nodded gently, listened to me vent and hummed quietly in understanding. "Have you ever heard of the term 'omnipresent'?"

I really wanted to scream at her in that moment. Here I was being serious, and she was about to dump some psychological crap on me and get into my head again. "No... but Doctor Lu-"

"Ironically, it is a characteristic of God, meaning to be

ever present. Everywhere. All of the time. Much like your husband in this manner. You see, sometimes our trauma can feel like that, ever present and everywhere. Do you like spiders, Kate?"

I had no idea where she was going with this, but I went with it anyway. What choice did I have really? "No, I hate spiders. They scare me."

"Right. It's funny, though, isn't it, when we don't like spiders, and we see one walking around in the house, but we lose sight of it? All of a sudden, it's gone, and we have no idea where. It becomes all we think about. We wait for it to pop out of nowhere, and we can't sleep because we can almost feel it crawling against our skin. The spider becomes omnipresent."

I began to laugh. "You're comparing God to a spider?"

Doctor Lucy, in turn, laughed at my comment. "No, Kate. I am comparing your husband to the spider. God becomes omnipresent because of faith; the spider becomes omnipresent out of fear. You want the truth? I think you're seeing Arlo in everything because you are afraid of dealing with the trauma he has left you with."

I hate to admit it, but what she was saying made some sense, and the fact that my eyes had begun to water as she spoke told me she was hitting something inside of me. She continued as I began to cry.

"You keep mentioning that he is asking you to write a book. What book, exactly?"

I shook my head. I had no idea what he was working on, only that it was religious in nature. "I wish I knew."

She thought briefly in silence, an idea bubbling away in her head. "I think we should find out and maybe it will help us both understand this situation a little better. Would you be up for doing that, Kate?"

I nodded gently and wiped my whole face against the course fabric of the straitjacket to dry my eyes. I just wanted it all to be over, and this was the way to do it.

Then so be it.

Chapter Eight

Saint Michael the Unseeing

I was kept in isolation for two days before I was finally released back into the madness of the Lodge. I knew Barty would be waiting for me, and I had no intention of speaking to him just yet. Thankfully, Michael was released from isolation on the same day. He was different. Like someone had sucked the life out of him. Physically, he was drawn and pale, and his facial hair had become scraggly, peppered with little white speckles. Emotionally, he was empty; you could see it in the way his shoulders hung lifelessly and that cold, never changing look in his eyes. He was lost. Maybe we all were. But if one person truly looked how they felt inside, it was Michael.

When we both left our isolation rooms, I had no idea what to say to Michael. Should I apologise to him? Did he even know that was Arlo he saw, and that he was my husband? He stood still after walking to my side. His eyes, of course, never met mine, but he knew I was there. His voice took me by surprise. He spoke quietly and weakly.

"What did you do to end up in heaven?"

I didn't understand what he meant by that, and at first, I was worried he had finally cracked, Barty the Behemoth style. It was only when he laughed and motioned back to the room to explain did I get his point.

"The soft room. All white, isn't it? Everything feels like a cloud, and you're just floating right in the middle of it all. It's a sick joke, but … some of us call it heaven."

"Oh. That makes sense, I guess." I walked closer to him as I continued talking. "Barty. Need I say more?"

Michael's signature smile emerged on his cheeks, but it wasn't his usual bright, room-lighting beam; it was barely even half of it. "He start up again and drag you with him?"

"Something like that." I hesitated before I asked the next part, checking to see if anyone was around to listen. "Michael, do you think we can go outside and talk?"

I knew he sensed trouble from the moment I asked, and truthfully, he had no reason to trust me and want to speak to me in private. He barely knew me, and really, who was trustworthy in a Lodge built for the mentally unstable? His brows turned to a slight, cautious frown, and his head tilted in my direction, similar to that of a confused dog. "I don't know if that's a good idea, Ka-"

"I know what you saw, Michael. I just don't want to get you into trouble and think it's best we talk alone."

I don't know how he did it, but he could always sense when someone was coming and how many people there were. Without warning, he grabbed my arm with his hand to use me as a guide and began walking down the corridor. Two nurses walked straight towards us, having just emerged from around the corner. Even I had no idea they would be there, but he somehow did.

"Breakfast? Good idea, Kate!" He had shouted it loud enough for anyone to hear, so any onlookers would assume we were going towards the canteen together for food.

The nurses had come to separate us and take us upstairs themselves, exactly as they were supposed to. I honestly thought we were busted until a voice down the hallway saved us.

"It's okay, I'm sure they can make their way to the canteen alone." Doctor Lucy was speaking directly to the two nurses as she flashed Michael and me a smile. "I will see you both later."

I gave her a small nod and continued walking along with Michael. Doctor Lucy had saved our backsides and had given us space to talk. But why? I never really understood whose side she was on and what her motives were. Did she know that Michael and I needed to talk? Was that a good idea in her eyes, or were we both about to spiral back into "heaven"?

As soon as we were out of earshot, we stopped, and Michael turned his body towards mine, remaining close so we didn't have to speak so loudly. "What do you mean you know *what* I saw, Kate?"

I sighed. There was really no way to sugar-coat this. "You saw a man in his late 40s, dark curly hair, throat slit ... right?"

Michael's expression wore concern. He even turned his head to look elsewhere, like he needed a distraction. His tongue was pressed against his cheek until he began to whisper back. "You know him? Was he really not in the room? Kate, I haven't seen anything in over a year, and yet I saw him and only him. Can you explain that? 'Cause I can't, and they think I'm crazy for it."

"You're not crazy. At least I don't think you are. I see him too." I sighed deeply before continuing this awkward confession. "His name is Arlo. He was my husband. I thought it was only me who could see him, but it turns out you can too. To make matters worse, Barty told me two days ago that both you and I can see him, and he knows about what Arlo and I speak about. It makes no sense, Michael. Unless this is some fucked up joint fever dream, I don't know what to say anymore."

Michael scoffed once, paused, then scoffed again. He backed up against the wall, and slowly slid down it until he was sat on the cold floor, laughing like this was the funniest thing ever. That was it, I thought; I finally pushed him over the edge. He was gone.

"Michael?"

He continued to laugh until tears ran down his cheeks and disappeared into his beard, like raindrops dying amongst the shrubbery of a forest. "I don't need this … not now. I have been trying so hard to just be *normal* so I can get home."

I moved to sit next to him on the floor as he spoke.

"I have a wife and three kids, and I have been told I cannot see them because I'm dangerous. Apparently, when I went blind, I 'assaulted' a man who was working on set. They arrested me, then Doctor Lucy came to get me. I haven't seen them since, and every day I do my best to prove I'm fine just so I can be with them again. Now you're saying I am seeing your dead husband?"

"I know, I know. I don't know why, and I am so sorry this is happening to you. Trust me, I don't want to be seeing him either."

He stayed quiet for about a minute and rubbed the leftover tears that lingered by his eyes. What he said next, I never expected to hear come from Michael's mouth.

"Did you kill him?"

It was so direct, and the fact he was the only one who hadn't judged me so far made it sting like salt to a wound. He must have sensed how much it hurt, because I felt his hand find my arm and squeeze it gently.

"You can tell me."

I turned to face him. He was looking straight at the blank wall across from us, the plaster featuring several shades of white. There was something about Michael that always made you feel at home, something that always made you feel safe. I thought back to how fortunate his wife must have felt to have him in her life, and, more painfully, wondered if Arlo ever was as understanding and supportive as this stranger had been to me.

"No. I didn't kill him."

It ended there. He didn't ask ever again, and he didn't question my answer. He just believed me like he had known me his whole life. I cannot begin to express how emotional it felt just for someone – anyone – to believe me. I leapt over and clung onto him, like my life depended on it. To my surprise, he hugged me back, and we both sat and cried for what felt like forever. We had both been accused of crimes we didn't commit, our whole lives had changed, and we had both lost everything overnight. Conveniently, Doctor Lucy had collected us both, and that made me wonder just how Barty ended up here too.

We both agreed that something didn't seem right, and together we would try and get to the bottom of it. But to really figure out what was going on and why, we needed an ally.

We needed Barty.

As agreed, I saw Doctor Lucy that night to touch base. She wanted to ensure both Michael and I were doing better and were safe to integrate back into the group. She saw us separately, of course, and we had both agreed to say nothing to her. We hadn't fully decided if she was trustworthy just yet, and we hadn't had a chance to speak with Barty either. Naturally, Barty came running to us both at breakfast to see how we were, his usual excited self. We told him to meet us both after our meeting, a perfect plan to meet up in my room to talk without prying eyes. Barty was on the same floor as me, so he could easily run back to his room; and Michael, well, he could always play the "I can't see and got lost" card.

It was a perfect plan.

"So, are you feeling a little better now, Kate?"

Doctor Lucy was sitting against my desk again, holding a bunch of papers.

"Yeah, I'm sorry I freaked out like that. I'm also sorry it may have fed into Barty's and Michael's psychoses. That wasn't fair."

She nodded gently and offered me a small smile. "Kate, we can only speak for our own actions. You have no need to apologise on behalf of Steven and Michael. They are responsible for their own actions. But I am glad you are feeling better, and I have something I would like to show you."

The papers she was holding were not what I thought

they were. I had assumed they were some kind of reports from all the patients she saw. How wrong was I. They were in a plastic-bag-like folder, taped with a word that had once been whole and untampered – EVIDENCE.

It was Arlo's work.

She handed it over to me without any hesitation. It was at least five hundred pages of typed writing, notes and even scribbles with pen. "I will leave this with you. The police weren't too happy to part with it, but I agreed to share any findings with them once you had it. I hope this can bring you some kind of closure, Kate."

Would it bring me closure? Was it worth opening this can of worms just to spread parasites everywhere?

Doctor Lucy had started to leave as I stopped her with my question. "What am I supposed to do with this?"

She paused at the door and turned back to me. Half of her body was shadowed from the darkness of the hallway. "What have you been told to do with it?"

Her smile resembled that of Arlo's in the shadows, and before I could figure out if that smile was genuinely hers, she was gone into the night.

I placed the evidence bag down at my desk and began to undo the packet, ready to expose the secrets within the papers.

"Omnibenevolence."

I jumped and looked back at the doorway Doctor Lucy had just walked through. Arlo emerged from it in her place.

"Meaning?"

He walked closer to look down at his own work. His fingers traced the plastic protecting his papers. "All-loving. Just like God is described as all-loving. Of everything and everyone. But is that true, Kate? Does God love everyone and everything? What about the ones who commit sin? Are they worth loving?"

I watched him look down at his work with an expression I had not expected. It was almost as if it was bittersweet to be back with the thing he had loved most.

I responded to him, "If God is all-loving, He is all-forgiving too. Sin doesn't matter as long as you can repent from it and move forward a better person."

He countered my comment with a question. "Can everyone admit they were wrong? Can everyone repent and move forward with God's approval?"

"Can you admit you were wrong?"

He paused and turned his eyes to me, searching my mind, my heart and my soul. "Wrong for attempting to complete my task? No. Wrong for hurting you? Yes. I should have told you the truth; I just didn't want you to suffer like I did. Now we have no choice but to work together."

His words held weight, and his apology meant everything to me. But I couldn't help but ask if it was far too late for love and niceties.

"On what exactly, Arlo? What is this?"

He opened the plastic and released the blood-stained pages onto the desk. His own blood on his own work. "This is the end. The one Barty has been speaking of. It's true, Kate. The End Day is coming, and only some will survive it."

He validated Barty, and Arlo had such a serious tone I wouldn't dare question him. If Arlo spoke it in such a way, it was most definitely the truth.

"And this book of yours, it's what exactly? The last

edition to holy scripture?"

Arlo nodded.

I had finally figured it out. The penny had dropped, and so did my stomach. "Arlo, you mean to say we are documenting the end of the world?"

"Do you know the story about Noah's Ark? Why that happened? God was unhappy with what humanity had become and had chosen to wipe the slate clean. Consider this round two; I just think fewer people will survive this one."

My heart had begun to race, and the blood whooshed around my head too fast. It pounded in my ears and made my body feel frozen. "What do you mean? You just said God was all-loving?"

Arlo smirked at me. "Was the Devil ever forgiven?"

Chapter Nine

Saint Arlo the Accuser

When Barty and Michael made their entrances into my room, they both jumped at the sight of Arlo standing next to me.

Barty spoke first. "If it isn't the messenger himself. Pleasure to formally meet you, Mr. Alonso."

Arlo smirked and looked back at me. I couldn't tell if he was basking in his fame, or if he just genuinely found Barty's behaviour to be as amusing as we all did. Michael looked at Arlo and swallowed the lump in his throat before speaking. "You're Arlo. I can see you …"

Arlo folded his arms like he always did, a mark of his impatience and lack of compassion. "Yes, yes, it's all very touching," he said spoke quickly, "but can we all agree we have more important matters to attend to?"

I moved in my chair and exposed the papers that were sitting at the desk. Barty gasped. He moved closer and touched some of the pages, despite how filthy they were.

"Is this it? The prophecy?"

I nodded. "This is everything Arlo wrote before he died. The problem is some of it doesn't make sense." I looked up at Arlo and sighed. "And he can't remember it."

Arlo rolled his eyes in response to my comment. "Can I remind you that I am dead? No longer living? Excuse me for not being able to remember everything before my untimely demise, Kate."

Barty mumbled to himself as he rummaged through some of the papers alongside Arlo. Michael, on the other hand, stood awkwardly observing the conversation. I was just about to ask Arlo if he was insinuating that I was the one who killed him, when Michael interjected before we could argue more. "So, are we all working together? Is that going to be an issue?"

Arlo gazed at Michael in an almost threatening way, a look that already questioned his statement before he even spoke. "Yes, we are working together, and if you are asking if Kate and I can work together, as husband and wife, yes we can."

I laughed at that and shook my head. "Husband and wife, that's funny." I snatched the papers from his hands and moved them away from his grip before I continued. "Look, I know we all have our differences, but I think we can all benefit from finding the hidden truth within these papers. About us, about all of this and why we are here. That means we work as a *team*, Arlo. You're not the boss. We are all equals in this. Understood?"

He hesitated, still agitated that I had taken his precious papers from him and shown him up in front of everyone, but he nodded. He had no choice. He either worked with us, or no one would ever know what it was he was trying to finish and why.

We had already met up for two nights in a row when we were sitting in my room, once again, asking Arlo questions as we looked at his papers. We had closed the door and were all sitting on the floor, quietly reading through section after section of Arlo's notes. The idea was to divide and conquer. The problem was Arlo's notes were as unhinged as he was. Even he couldn't understand his own ramblings. Words were scribbled in unruly, doctor-like handwriting, like prescriptions you would have to guess at. They weren't even consistent. Some would start on one page and end up on another. It was a nightmare. The worst part was the fact the police had managed to completely jumble the order of his work, and since smarty pants Arlo didn't number his pages, we had to guess where everything went. It was like attempting to complete a cheap puzzle from a battered box, not knowing if all the pieces were there, or if they even belonged to the same puzzle for that matter. Ironically, just like the puzzle I had thrown at Arlo days prior.

His work consisted of passages and passages on the human condition, the ways humans had changed and how religion was misconceived. I had never known Arlo to question religion or its effect on anyone. He was never religious despite the fact he was born into a religious household. Catholic. Every single one of them. He hated it. In fact, I remember when we got engaged, he mentioned that his mother would have forced us into marrying in a church if she were still in his life. I never so much minded. To me, it was always a matter of respect rather than a statement. I only met his parents twice, and after that, Arlo abandoned every member of his family. The weight of family was heavier than fame, and he wanted *balance*.

The passages themselves started out as opinion but slowly drifted into fact and later became prophecy. Towards the end of it all, his notes narrowed down to an implication that an apocalypse was upon us. No doubt the one Barty had been speaking of. The problem was, as his notes became more erratic, he began to draw in symbols and letters not known to man. These were the pages we all agreed to place in a separate pile and consider useless.

Barty looked up from his papers and glanced at Arlo. He wanted to ask him something, and I knew Barty well enough by now to know he would just blurt it out. "Arlo? Why did you start working on this? When did God tell you to write this?"

Arlo was reading with his glasses hanging from his nose, listening to Barty but never looking at him. "It came to me in a dream. I fell asleep one night, and I was spoken to. I was told about what was to come and that I was to document it all."

Barty nodded in understanding, but he wanted more than just a simple answer. "Did God tell you this was going to happen? When I had my accident, I saw the end of the world. All of it. The way it happens and why."

Surprisingly, Arlo placed his paper down and looked up at us all before speaking. "All I know is the End Day is coming, and I was just told to write it all down. For the future to see? For whoever survives to learn from? For God himself? I don't know. I just know it wasn't finished, and a part of the prophecy is either hidden in these texts or missing."

Michael sighed, his job always being redundant because he couldn't read the pages set in front of him, but he asked the question we had all been thinking: "So, if you were writing it, and you know all about it, why do you need us now to help you with it? Shouldn't you be talking to God about it?"

"Amen," Barty chipped in. "By his words."

Arlo became still, almost in shock of Michael's question. It was either that, or he had realised just how crazy the people around him were as he looked at me for help. I lifted my hands up as if to say I wasn't helping him out here.

"I haven't heard from God since I died. I wasn't meant to die before it was done."

"Radio silence on your end, and you just assume we are here to help you? I'm sorry, but what the hell has this got to do with us?"

Barty went to protest Michael's use of the word "hell" but stopped as Michael apologised briefly. He was more concerned with Arlo's answer, and I, too, was curious.

"Because I was told if anything were to happen to me that Kate would be the one to take over. I had assumed by now she would have had some intervention or something! I didn't invite you two, by the way; that was all Kate. You want to leave? Leave."

I waited for Michael's and Barty's reactions, half expecting them to get up and leave. They owed me nothing, and they didn't have to be involved in this. Doctor Lucy had just suggested that I go through this process to better myself. This truly had nothing to do with them.

I chimed in after Arlo, clearing the awkward silence between us all. "Arlo's right. You don't have to be here, and you don't have to do this. You all have your own issues and your own problems to deal with. I don't want to be a hindrance to any of you. Doctor Lucy thinks this is what's best for me, but I can't say the same for you. Please, do what's right for you."

As if instantly, I felt Barty's hand touch my knee. He was smiling deeply at me. "You're our friend, Kate. We will be here for you. Won't we, Michael?"

Michael nodded without thought and offered me a smile.

Arlo watched us all and added, "I think you're all so lucky for ending up together. If it weren't for Doctor Lucy, you wouldn't be here to support one another through your darkest hour. Things didn't turn out the way we had hoped, but maybe we can work it out together. The world is ending, and I, for one, would like to know when and how. Wouldn't you?"

We all nodded in agreement. If the world was ending, we most definitely wanted to know when and how.

Arlo left soon after our conversation. We were all tired and had gotten nowhere with our investigation thus far. We were all sitting on the floor in our usual circle, deep into the hours of the morning. That was the first time we had been alone, just us three. No staff, no Doctor Lucy and no Arlo. It was a free space, and we spoke openly about how our lives once were, and what they had become.

Michael spoke about his wife and his wonderful children. How much he had missed them all and how he hadn't seen them in what felt like forever. He confessed that he had already missed birthdays and a Christmas, and those were things he would never get back. That broke my heart to hear, but I was happy Michael had us to talk to about it. Instead of ignoring his family's existence to try and feel less pain, we encouraged him to talk about them more, so they still felt a part of his life.

Barty spoke about his troubled youth and the trouble he used to get in. The amount of times he had been arrested was astonishing, and his old lifestyle was not what you'd expect from the man sitting before us. He really was a wild child, one that completely removed his family from his life because of how awfully they had treated him growing up. He had a past – no doubt a shit ton of trauma to go with it – and I remember feeling grateful that Barty had shared his experiences with us, because I knew it must have been hard to admit half of his flaws.

I told them both how I met Arlo, and how, once upon a time, we had a good life together. I then opened up about how crap our relationship had become, and how it led to us living under the same roof but not seeing one another. They were surprised, to say the least, that I had not yet had a life of my own, that my husband had managed to stomp on any chance I had of a career for his own.

Both Barty and Michael listened to me. They didn't judge me, they didn't make me feel unimportant, and they actually offered some advice and support. I remember asking myself that night where they had been my whole life. When we first met, we had hastily made assumptions about one another. Me especially. I had come to realise I had no right to do that, and they were both exceptional individuals. In another life, we could have been sitting in the back garden of one of our mansions right now, all with our significant others, drinking beer and laughing all night long. The summer nights would never end, and our friendship would outlast us all. It was a beautiful thought, but we were sitting on the floor of an asylum.

We gave one another warm smiles, and the laughter faded as the night drew to a close. We all had that sickening feeling that this was what life could have been for us. The sweet moments we had shared talking turned sour as we called it a night, and once I was alone, I cried.

When I had wanted my life to change, this is exactly what I had asked for. I just wished it was under better circumstances. But that was life, right?

Bittersweet.

Chapter Ten

The All-Knowing

The next night, we all agreed, as always, to meet up in my room. We all had different roles, and we were each tasked with a job earlier that day. Michael was to steal a few crayons from drawing class so we could begin marking the pages we were going through. I was to divide the pages into clear sections so we could better understand what we were going through, a piece at a time. Barty, well we may have given him a job that wasn't necessary just to keep him quiet. He had become so animated about us working on proving his theory correct that we had begged him to revise the Bible to teach us later on – just so he wouldn't tell the whole asylum we were working on something sacred.

Barty and I were sitting inside my room when Michael arrived. He announced his entrance with his success. "I think I got the red ones." He held up the crayons he had stolen from one of our classes, proud of his thieving skills. But he wasn't going to become the world's best shoplifter anytime soon, because the crayons were not red at all.

Arlo screwed his face up then smacked his head. "They're blue … not red."

I watched Arlo belittle Michael, and, truthfully, it really

pissed me off. The worst part was Michael could actually see Arlo's negative expression. I wasn't having any of it.

"He's blind, you dickhead. He can't see what colour it is!" I took a crayon from Michael and pointed it at Arlo. "What does it matter, anyway? It can write, can't it? Or maybe you're the blind one who can't see blue?"

Arlo sniggered in a mocking way and circled around the desk to be beside Barty, his only ally. The only person willing to glorify him.

As always, we had organised ourselves to read over sections of Arlo's work, going back over his nonsense in search of something. Anything.

"Arlo, what is all of this? None of this makes any sense. It is like word vomit. I thought you were an amazing writer who was worth millions?"

He answered me without lifting his gaze from the page he was reading. "Have you ever heard about speaking in tongues?"

"Yes, but that's *speaking,* not writing."

Arlo slammed his papers down onto the floor and looked at me. "Do you really think I know how the Holy Spirit works? Like I chose to do this? God didn't exactly say, 'Oh hey, Arlo, do you fancy writing the next Bible?' Did he?"

Barty nodded frantically and added to the debate. "God works in mysterious ways. But God is omniscient. He knows everything, and what He knows and plans is what we should trust and believe in. Amen."

I grunted and shook my head. His point wasn't helpful to this conversation at all. "Let me guess, did Doctor Lucy tell you that? She loves her 'omni' crap."

Barty nodded, and Arlo smirked as he went back to his reading his page.

"Doctor Lucy is one fine, intelligent and independent woman," Arlo remarked.

That really sparked me up. How dare he talk about another woman like that in front of me. "Oh yeah, well you should have married her then, hey? Maybe you'd even be alive still!"

"I think I found it!" Michael looked up in our direction and happily flagged a piece of paper over his head.

We all stared at him blankly. What did he *find* exactly?

He looked at the paper he was holding and smiled. "The notes about the End Day? Isn't that what we were looking for?"

Arlo frowned and examined the paper he was holding. It was one covered in the gibberish he had scribbled and put to the side, a useless piece that had been thrown in the no-go pile. "There is nothing on here but meaningless scribbles and symbols, Michael."

Michael frowned deeply, his brows almost covering half of his eyes. He traced his fingers over the page and began to read. "When the day arrives, it will be set that three men and one woman shall fall. Together they hold the book of knowing from the evil that seeks it. This will mark the start of the end. Humanity will fall by its own hand."

We all stopped to listen to Michael read. He was the only one who understood any of the mess Arlo had jotted down. Even Arlo was at a loss for words.

"You can read that?"

Michael nodded in confusion. "Can't you?"

We all replied at once. "No."

"Oh. Well, that's pretty neat."

It was "pretty neat." It was also suspiciously convenient that Arlo had pre-emptively written notes that only Michael could read, like he knew we would end up here. I stared at Arlo as he began to sort through his papers excitedly, fishing out all the ones with Michael's secret language on them. He was excited to get to the bottom of his work, but I felt a sick feeling come to my stomach like something was really wrong. Why would anyone be so excited to watch humanity end? Even Barty, who knew this was coming, looked as if he might collapse in disgust.

Barty spoke quietly. "Three men and one woman ... is that us?"

Arlo's mind began to tick, just like his typewriter used to, and a look of obsession crossed his face. I didn't like where this was going, and something inside of me told me to stop.

I spoke out abruptly. "Maybe we should call it a night? It's getting really late, and I don't want Barty and Michael to get into trouble."

Arlo paused and shot me a look filled with filth, like I had spat on his face. "Why would we stop when we are so close?"

I saw the fire in his eyes, the anger that sat within him, and I knew that even Michael and Barty could feel his rage. There was something about his demeanour that scared me. Arlo was an angry man, but the fury he shot at me then felt different, threatening. I did the only thing I could do in that moment. I compromised.

"I am not suggesting we stop. I am suggesting we let Michael go and read these in his room, and tomorrow we can meet up and discuss his findings in the rec room?"

Barty yawned, and Michael nodded in agreement with me. Thankfully, they backed me up.

Arlo assessed the room and suddenly smiled, a complete shift in character. "Of course."

He reluctantly handed Michael all of the pages he had to read and began gathering the rest to neatly place back into the evidence bag. I watched him handle the papers and remembered how he used to work. Arlo would sometimes rip whole pages out of scripts, tear through them, and tape new pieces together. I even once saw him set fire to a whole manuscript. This time, however, he cradled his work like a newborn baby, his greatest creation in life. It felt unsettling and unfamiliar.

I began to rise up from the floor as I spoke, my voice slightly shaky. "I … I'm going to walk Barty back to his room … and make sure Michael gets to the stairs okay."

Arlo didn't even look at me as he continued to smooth out his pages and order them. "Okay, we will meet tomorrow in the rec room at 9 a.m. sharp. After breakfast. Understood?"

I just grabbed Michael's arm and, with Barty following behind, replied simply, "Yes."

We got out into the hallway and firmly shut the door behind us to conceal ourselves from Arlo. Something felt off, and even Barty was quiet, which was not normal. We stayed in silence till we got to Barty's door. Michael and I pushed him inside to speak in a whisper.

"Michael, I really need you to read this all tonight, but whatever you do, don't tell Arlo what you find before talking to us. I don't trust him."

Barty looked at me with concern and touched my shoulder. "Kate, I will never question the word of God, but there is something about your husband that doesn't sit with faith. I knew the end of the world was upon us, and I agree that knowing when and how is crucial if it is God's will for us to know it. But like I was trying to say earlier, God is omniscient. He is all-knowing but that doesn't mean we should be too. Man has known things that have destroyed populations, like how to construct weapons, such as the nuclear bomb. God gave us knowledge to better ourselves, not cause war. If Arlo is a soldier of God and was chosen to deliver this message, then why is he himself not all-knowing of His plan? Why is he so desperate to find a truth that God has tried to conceal?"

As nuts as Barty was – and he was nuts – what he said that night made so much sense. Even Michael and I felt the gravity of his words. I am unsure how Arlo himself, who had been so self-absorbed in his own work, no longer remembered what he was working towards and needed us to figure it out for him.

"I agree with you, Steven." I nodded and placed my hand on his shoulder. "I think it was intended for Michael to know and not for Arlo to remember."

Michael sighed as he clutched onto the papers, his wristband with his patient ID rubbing against them. Regardless of everything, we were still tagged like little rats in a cage. "I will read it all tonight. Tomorrow we will skip breakfast and talk in the rec room before Arlo shows up. Maybe then, we will know exactly what we are dealing with."

I agreed with Michael and so did Barty. We parted ways for the night, and I had to make my way back to my room before Arlo grew suspicious of our plans. Michael had agreed to read all night, while Barty wished to pray for guidance. I, on the other hand, had to play the role I was born to play: a dumb, dependent woman.

Arlo was placing the final page back into its place as I entered the room. "Did Michael get off okay?" were his first words to me, his only interest.

"Yeah, he won't get caught, and I'm sure he will read it all before tomorrow."

Arlo nodded and closed the bag, turning his gaze to me. "Good, it is crucial he does."

I nodded and awkwardly stood at the door, unsure if I was willing to walk past him to get into bed, but Arlo had already walked up to me, his expression stern.

His hand rose, and I didn't flinch, not even as his palm held my cheek. He spoke quietly now and close to my lips. I felt a mixture of anxiety and excitement pulse through me. "You have no idea how important you have been in all of this. You were always that missing puzzle piece that connected the picture together."

His smile was chilling, and his hand slipped from my face, down my neck and all the way across my body until it met with my waist. My breathing slowed, and I could feel my heart thumping through my chest as he pulled me closer and began to dance around the room with me. I followed him and his movements like a doll on strings, obedient and ever controlled.

"Kate, you will be known by all as the woman who made this happen. A woman who needn't power, presence, love or knowledge to complete the task."

He swirled me around as he spoke, and even tipped me back in his hold. His dark eyes pierced through mine. He brought me closer to him once more, his lips now grazing mine as he spoke.

"You are my most loyal servant."

And with that he was gone. I was alone.

I began to whimper in fear. I knew the man I had married; I may not have known the man he became, but if I knew anything, it was that Arlo had two left feet.

He couldn't dance.

Chapter Eleven

The Holy Trinity

Sleep would not take me after Arlo's touch. I had been left with so many questions and no answers. As the sunlight crept in through the window, I knew that day would be my last in the Lodge. Don't ask me how; I just knew it. I had this feeling deep inside of me that the inevitable was about to occur, and that if anyone amongst Barty, Michael or I would have to make a sacrifice, then I should be the one to do it. Barty may have been crazy, but his intentions were pure, and Michael had a family he was dying to get back to. I, on the other hand, had nothing left, and nothing to lose.

The events of that night began to change us, and it became noticeable from the moment we left my room. Barty was thinking more clearly and acting less animated, and regardless of his undying faith, he was being smart and cautious about the situation. Michael himself had started becoming accustomed to looking at and speaking with us as if he had started seeing again. Even I was feeling less like I was crazy and began to accept reality for what it was, regardless of the circumstances and wrong accusations on me. I was starting to take control of my own future. I wanted to know who Arlo was and why he was so desperate to use us.

I made my way down to the rec room on the premise I was going for breakfast, just as we had agreed in private. Barty's room was empty as I passed it. I only hoped he was already downstairs with Michael. Everyone I passed was quiet that morning and working like clockwork, just as they always were, caught up in their routines as if in a scripted play, always playing their parts perfectly. The only ones who didn't fit the bill that morning were us three. We were breaking the status quo, so to speak. We were the ones jeopardising the well-oiled machine around us, the spanner about to be thrown in the works.

The rec room was empty except for Barty and Michael, who were already sat at the activities table. That room always had an unhinged feel to it, but now that it didn't house its usual foray of madness, it felt even stranger. I could sense that they were both troubled from the offset; it was written on both of their faces, and Barty was unusually quiet. I pulled up a chair to sit with them. We were seated in the same circle we were sat in on the first day we met, a full circle in our journey together. It truly did feel like the end.

Barty spoke first. "Kate, Michael has some information for us."

I nodded and looked over at Michael, who was holding a stack of papers, the ones he was meant to read over last night. "I have something to tell you both too. Last night, after we parted ways, Arlo was... different." I sighed in between my words, playing with my fingers nervously. "That's not Arlo. Whoever we have been working with – *for* – is not who we think they are."

Michael nodded, placed the papers down and flicked through them to find one in particular. He placed a single finger down on the page, highlighting a date that was roughly written in blue crayon. "I found it, Kate. What he was looking for. It's the day the world ends."

I leant over to look at what Michael was talking about, confused as to why a singular date would mean so much. "But why is the date so important? I don't understand?"

Michael began skimming through the papers once more, pulling them out one by one. "It says here that the day of the apocalypse was to be written by the first saint on the instruction of God himself. That God had ordered the saint to do so, as He was unhappy with how humanity had changed. He wanted a do-over, just like Arlo said yesterday. But what he didn't mention was the rest of it. God never wanted to execute this plan. In fact He sought to destroy the work because He had come to realise that wiping out humanity to start over wouldn't change a thing. He wanted to give us all a second chance. But someone had other ideas and still wanted to execute the plan. They just needed three more things to do it."

He spread three sheets out on the table before us and began to explain further. Michael pointed at the first sheet and started. "A saint that would be found during his darkest hour, one that would rise up and praise God, denouncing his sinful ways. He will work as the messenger of the coming apocalypse."

My eyes darted over to Barty as Michael's finger moved to the next.

"A saint that would lose everything, including his vision, so that he is able to see the things man has fallen blind to. He will be the translator of scripture of the coming apocalypse."

I swallowed the developing lump in my throat as I heard

his finger trace over to the next paper.

"A saint that will make a sacrifice to change her life, a sacrifice that will bind her into chains of loyalty so that she may become strong enough to lead the others. She will be ... the herald of the coming apocalypse."

Michael moved back from his space as Barty stared at me with his deep blue eyes. My skin felt chilled, and reality felt like a distant memory. It felt as if someone had pulled the rug from under my feet, and I was thrown aimlessly through the air, awaiting my inevitable fall. They didn't have to say a word. It all became so clear, so quickly.

We were the saints of Arlo's scripture.

I licked the moisture back into my lips and spoke softly. The power drained from my muscles. "If God didn't want this to happen, then why is it? Why are we here?"

Michael went to speak, but Barty placed a hand on his shoulder to stop him. He clearly wanted to explain his theory himself. "The night of my accident, I changed. I felt God's grasp on me, Kate. God had given me a second chance to live, and I had never felt more alive. I was weightless. Free. I woke up in the hospital, and there she was – Doctor Lucy. She told me she was sent to protect me from people who wouldn't understand, and she brought me here. She never once called me crazy, and she would have me repeat my prophecy on the coming apocalypse. She was fascinated by it and told me she, too, was one of God's soldiers. Michael, too, was collected by Doctor Lucy before he was even arrested. She promised to protect him and help him find his way back to his family. She never had his blindness tested and believed that Michael was *gifted*. She paired us both together as soon as he arrived here."

I listened to him carefully before interjecting my question. "Then me? She collected me … the fourth saint?"

Barty nodded and reached over to hold my hand carefully. "You were the final piece of the puzzle. She collected you too. We've been used, Kate. By a woman who does not believe in God, but opposes Him. She wants the world to end, of that, I'm sure."

We all remained quiet for a moment, digesting the horrific revelations we had just learned. We had been collected. Like stamps for a book. Like tools for a box. Like saints for an apocalypse. The mercy we thought we had been shown was a lie. Everything was a lie. The worst part was we had successfully managed to fulfil three-quarters of the task. The last part, however, had fallen to me.

"I am going to end the world?"

Michael's head dropped in sympathy, clearly knowing something I didn't.

"Michael, what does it say? What am I going to do?"

He lifted his head to look in my direction, his blind gaze focused on the space between us. "I don't know … Arlo didn't finish it."

As the cold truth trickled its way down our spines and planted our feet to the floor, an emotionlessness feeling settled in. We were useless now. All we knew was that I was the key to the end of the world, but we didn't know how. I, Katherine Alonso, a woman of nothing, was everything.

I felt them hold a hand of mine each. Their warmth attempted to keep me there with them in that moment. But all I could think about was how I was the designated bringer of death. That in some sick, twisted turn of fate, I was the one who hadn't lived a full life of my own, but I was to take everyone else's. I held on to their hands tightly, not wanting to leave them. They had been my crutches. My support. My world.

"I'm sorry …"

We heard a loud clapping fill the empty room, throwing us all back into horror, the tender moment of safety over.

The truth we had searched for so desperately had found us as we found it. It stood at the doorway clapping.

It came to take from us once more.

Chapter Twelve

Saint Katherine the Pariah

Arlo was standing at the doorway, clapping loudly, with a gigantic smile plastered over his face. "Congratulations, you finally figured it out." He began to walk closer to us. "You have the key to the end."

We all stared at him silently, and a newfound fear took over us as he stopped halfway into the room and continued to speak.

"You know, I really couldn't have done it without you three. Well, four, but Arlo isn't here to thank, is he Kate? You saw to that yourself." He chuckled to himself, amused with his proclamation.

His gaze flicked over towards Barty. "Barty, Barty, Barty. You truly are the most religious man I know, and it is so … disappointing! You were *mine*. You worshipped *me*. You revelled in the shadows of sin, and yet one little knock to the head ended everything, and you became *His* truest disciple once more. That religious upbringing you had stuck to your soul real good, didn't it, Barty? I knew He would come to collect you that day. He would forgive you for all of it and offer you a place up there. But no, I got to you first."

He stepped one step closer as his hair grew longer and

his face became smoother, more feminine. Arlo was slowly morphing into Doctor Lucy, and all was becoming clear. His voice changed from its familiar huskiness as he continued to speak, the tone shifting like a hand running up piano keys, and a strong woman's voice emerged.

"Michael Gray. You pathetic man. Do you know how I found this one, Kate? He was spending all of his hard-earned money on the weak — all the blind, worthless fuckers who walk the earth — because he himself had been touched by the role he played. His wife and children are just as *perfect* as he was. But they had no idea the price he paid to get there, did they Michael? I gave you power, fame and a life! Sin made you; and you, you ungrateful little whelp, changed sides. So, I took it all away from you — those eyes of yours, your family, and then your life. You killed yourself, you know? You became so hysteric, I watched as you provoked your own death. The ironic thing is, you were so blind you practically took my hand over His."

Her laugh was piercing, and her eyes finally settled on me. Her complexion became warmer. "And you, Kate. I will confess you weren't my first choice, but I missed Arlo. *He* got to him first. And although I was gutted by the outcome, I saw an opportunity with you. You were mine, anyway, after you had killed Arlo. You committed a sin even too great for *Him* to forgive, but He still tried to take you. Your contract was written as soon as you drew that knife over your husband's throat, and what joy I had throwing it in His face when I came for you. Oh, don't look so surprised, Kate. You must have known it was you all this time?"

I felt my whole body turn numb. A sick realisation settled in.

"You really don't remember, do you? Pity. You enjoyed it, you know? Killing him. I did need him, though, and I had been working hard at unpicking that brain of his. Another week or so, and I am sure he would have taken his own life. But you had other plans I didn't see coming. I saw your hatred for him, for the god he had begun to love, and you were just so easy to manipulate. Women have changed so much over the centuries, and you, you just remained weak. All I had to do was become the one person you surrendered yourself to – Arlo."

I spoke for all of us. "Arlo was never here. You collected us all so we could give you the end of the world ..."

"Isn't she smart? But too little, too late. You really still haven't figured out who I am? And why I want the world to end?"

Michael let go of my hand and stepped forward. His irises contracted as Doctor Lucy became a bright shade of red. "I know exactly who you are. I see exactly what you are." He stepped closer to her as her features began to change. "You are Lucifer. You are the Devil."

The creature in front of us all was even visible to Michael, crimson skinned and horned, and almost beast-like from the waist down. Despite its red hue, it was filthy and marked in some places, like it had rolled around in dirt. It was scarred, and several slash marks could be seen throughout its tough, thick, leathery skin. Thick, black hair hung around its neck, waist and ankles; it was like a trophy of slaughtered animals proudly flashing its owner's successes in battle. Its horns and outstretched wings are what terrified me the most. The books always said the horns of the Devil were goat-like, but that was far from the truth. They were agonisingly crippled in different directions and sharp at every point. The torn, bare wings of the beast were a reminder of what it once was: an angel. How could something so pure become so corrupt? The visage of Lucifer was terrifying, yes, but in some terms, agonising to look at. Could we all become just as horrific? Maybe our souls already were.

Its breath was hot like fire as it spoke once more. "Doctor Lucy – Lucifer. I really thought someone would have noticed sooner." It scoffed and sat on the sofa with one leg draped over the other, hooves on show. "You see, the thing is, I have been straight with all of you. Your opinions are all your own. I never influenced them. Even God himself knows how flawed humanity is, and I didn't prophesy an ending. He did. But He took some kind of pity on you all, as He always does, and He scrapped the idea. Your husband wrote it all down in his little riddles, and God chickened out because He felt you all deserved your second chance."

The creature paused and played with its long fingernails, laughing to itself. "You always get forgiven; that's just how it goes. But me? No. Never. I wanted it all to end, His perfect little creations. I am so sick and tired of dealing with all of His broken rejects and all I wanted was to take from Him what He loves most."

I understood how it felt. To feel like the one you were most loyal to and loved unconditionally had stripped you of everything because they loved something more than you. Right under your nose, like you never mattered. Like you were a test, the first mistake, that would lead on to better things. Arlo had made me feel that way. As God had made the Devil feel that way. I knew what it sought, and I spoke it aloud.

"Revenge."

It glared at me with a smirk. It was impressed with my observation, almost proud of the lust for a revenge I apparently carried out on my husband. "And that is why you ended up mine, Kate. We are not so different."

It stood up and started to walk around us, circling us. "You consider yourself 'saints,' the four humans chosen to protect humanity from a fate already written. You will be so much more now you are mine. You will be the four pillars of the coming apocalypse: conquest, war, famine and death. The work is already done. It is time."

We were all stunned by the revelations spoken by this demon, but even more terrified by the fact we had so stupidly been working the with Devil herself. Himself? I had no idea anymore.

Out of all three of us, it was Barty who was brave enough to make the first move. He stepped forward, away from me and beyond Michael, until he was face to face with the beast. "I don't serve you. I will never serve you. You will never have my soul …"

The demon laughed. The sound did not resemble that of man or woman; it was deep and unnatural, and a forked tongue peeked from between the Devil's lips. "You will follow a god so ready to sacrifice you all for his own gain? Instead of joining me and having the power of conquest? Is it not you who wanted to be a prophet before your death? Influencing every country your music would touch?"

"That is not who I am anymore. You will have no influence over me!" Barty then did the craziest thing I have ever seen him do. He had spoken a lot, shouted the place down, and sometimes sang and danced around the tables; but that morning, he leapt straight onto the Devil that stood before him and attempted to subdue it.

Michael and I took our chance, not wanting to waste the window Barty had given us. We hastily gathered the papers that were left on the table, not wanting to hand any of them over, and ran. We may have been many things in our lifetimes, but we were not the bringers of the End Times.

Barty screamed loudly, making us both halt. When I turned back to see why he had made that noise, he was being lifted into the air by his throat, overpowered by the demon. I was just about to run and help him. How? I didn't know. I just didn't want him to suffer. But what happened next brought Michael and me to our knees.

The horned beast roared loudly as it flung Barty against the wall. "So, you wish to be the Messiah? Have it your way, pathetic preacher." It reached up and agonisingly snapped its own two horns from its forehead, then once again lifted Barty to the wall. The Devil pierced through both of Barty's hands with the newly weaponised horns and pinned him up against the rec room mural. His bloodied body looked as if it hung from the knowledge tree in Eden as he whimpered in agony. He had finally become the image of what he had wanted to be: Jesus.

Barty weakly lifted his head to look at us both through his long curls stained with blood. Then he did the unthinkable – he smiled. Like his job had been done and the battle was over. I watched him take his last breath, and I never expected to feel as much love for him as I did in that moment. The guilt that welled up inside reduced me to tears, but what I felt was nothing less than respect and compassion towards a man who had selflessly sacrificed himself for me, for us.

I would have stayed there and continued to weep if it weren't for Michael lifting me off the ground with a harsh yank of the arm. He dragged me across the floor until I got to my feet, and we both began to run frantically through the never-ending halls of the Lodge. Michael didn't make any sound. His expression was blank, and his only mission was to get us both away from the disgusting demon that had just crucified Barty.

"Michael?" He was still pulling my arm and running as I cried, trying to get his attention. "Michael …"

He pulled on me harder, urging me to keep up. But we had been unsuccessful, running in a circle throughout the barren halls of the Lodge. It was no use. It was the Devil's playground, and right now we were just making this fun.

"MICHAEL!"

He finally stopped, panting , his eyes wide and frantic.

"There is no point running. It's over." I watched him as his face contorted into a fit of tears. "Michael, it's okay. It's over."

He continued to cry as we heard the beats of demon hooves clanking against the hard floor, mirroring that of Doctor Lucy's heels. Michael shook his head and handed me the papers he had smuggled from the table before Barty's death. He spoke softly. "I know it's over for us, Kate. But it doesn't have to be for everyone. Go, destroy it … before it's too late."

I stared at him, and for the first time ever, Michael looked at me, straight into my eyes.

"What are you going to-"

"I am not important. Forget about me. Go."

"But Michael … no."

The clinking of hooves drew closer.

"Yes. This is how it's meant to be ... please ..."

I hesitated, not wanting to leave him, unsure of what it was he wanted me to do. But as the sound grew eerily close, he shouted and pushed me away.

"GO!"

I fled, back towards my bedroom, and never looked back. As I ran for my life, there was silence in the desolate halls, an unsettling silence that was cut by Michael's blood-curdling scream. I never knew what happened to him; I just prayed it was nothing like Barty's death. His scream had marked time. I knew he was gone, but I also knew I was next.

I slammed the door closed behind me and began frantically searching for anything I could destroy the manuscript with. But this place was, in all its glory, an asylum. There was nothing sharp I could use to cut the pages. Nothing like a lighter I could set them on fire with. The only weapon I had was the singular blue crayon that Michael had left me. So, I did what I could, scribbling over every page, one by one, covering them all in blue crayon. I tore some of the pages and even crumpled some up desperately. It was no use. Whatever I did, the writing would still be visible. The crayon was weak, the tears could be matched up, and I am sure the Devil could straighten out any crinkles with ease. I was failing, and as I continued to try and work through all the pages Michael had given me, a voice made me jump.

"You really think that's going to stop the coming apocalypse?"

There he was – Arlo. I knew it wasn't him, but it had taken his form to mock me, to torture me and to provoke me.

"Kate, my dear ... you wanted this as much as I did. Don't you remember our conversations? About how corrupt the world is and how Arlo destroyed your life? You made this happen, and now you want to go back? To what?"

It changed back into Doctor Lucy. "You're a powerful woman, Kate. We don't need these men to finish the task. We can do it, just us two. As women." It edged closer to me as I held the last sheet of paper to my chest, its page hot and full of information I had a choice of sharing. "Eve was the smart one. She listened to me because she, too, knew that men were incapable of running the show. She didn't want to live in the shadow of Adam. She knew women, for centuries to come, would end up like her if she didn't act. Women just like you, who suffered from men like Arlo. Eden was a lie, just like your world, Kate. Let us end it together! If it's all gone, no one else has to suffer."

I listened to it speak, taking in every word. I had stopped, and a part of me, however wrong, was considering taking its offer. The world was a shit place. The world didn't need the four bringers of the apocalypse; they were already among us. Humans had become fixated on starting wars to conquer populations, leaving trails of death and famine behind them. The world was already on the path to self-destruction. Maybe choosing to end it all would be the lesser of two evils. A mercy.

"Come on, Kate. Hand me over the key, the date on which we can finally exact justice for ourselves on our abusers. Finally have our revenge on my father and your husband. *You* ... and *me*."

Its hand was held out towards me, calmly waiting for

the *key* that I clung to my chest. My eyes dared to connect with the Devil's as I braced myself for what was to come. I made a decision. It wasn't the Devil's, it wasn't God's, and it wasn't Arlo's. It was mine.

"No."

Its face shifted from its serious, sympathetic act, back to a power-hungry smirk. "Pity. I thought you were like Eve."

"No. I guess centuries of being pushed around by the Devil made women smarter."

I started to tear the paper in my hand as its expression changed from controlled to panicked. It leapt towards me in a flurry, a desperate attempt to grab the paper from me, as it reverted to its beast form. In its eagerness, the Devil tore through what it desired so deeply. I felt sharp, agonising nails pierce through me, just as easily as they had torn through the paper between us. Everything felt still in that moment as I bled onto the white floor, through my white clothes and into my white soul. I was dying.

The Devil stood in front of me, but I did not scream. It removed its hand from my stomach, confused by my stillness but respecting my strength. And then it vanished. The battle was over. First Barty, then Michael, and finally, me. All of us had been manipulated, tricked and used. But now it was over. Now we would wither away like the flowers the Lodge was built upon. But did we win or lose? Was the world about to end? I didn't know, and in my final moment, I didn't care.

I fell to the floor, surrounded by Arlo's pages. They blanketed me in some sickening comfort as I knew I lay on my death bed. Was it his twisted way of saying he was here? Right at the end? I gazed up at the ceiling I had fallen asleep looking at for weeks now. Yet as I looked up, I could see all the origami cranes had begun to flap their wings in unison. The wind flowed from their wings in freedom, no longer bound to their flightless, paper bodies. It was then I smiled. I knew it was over.

I was no longer bound.

I was no longer crazy.

I was dead.

Chapter Thirteen

Exit-dus

The police officers' heavy boots trod carefully down the rugged hallways as they made their way up the stairs. Agnes had informed them that Arlo always worked upstairs in the loft. She had called them when she found the bodies that morning, a wonderful way to start her day. When they finally reached Arlo's office door, it was cracked slightly open, and they could already smell it. Arlo Alonso was dead.

Agnes sat at the counter in the kitchen, speaking with a detective. They in no way suspected her for any of this crime. After all, they had no reason to. The moment they found Kate's body on the floor of her art room, they started to put the puzzle pieces together.

Agnes couldn't remove the thought from her mind. The way Kate lay in a pool of blood, pages scattered around her. At first, it seemed almost sacrificial; all that was missing were the candles and salt shapes. There were obvious signs that they both were killed with a knife, most likely the one that was conveniently missing from its holder in the kitchen. Agnes was blaming herself for the whole ordeal. She knew Kate was unhappy, but she never knew she was capable of committing such a crime.

The detective spoke to her as she sobbed. "Did Mrs. Alonso ever show any violence towards Mr. Alonso?"

She shook her head. It was the truth; she didn't. "No, but they were both very unhappy. I knew they argued a lot, and Mr. Alonso forced us all into signing an agreement to never speak of their family's business to anyone. Actually, I don't know if I am even allowed to tell you this …"

The detective placed a hand on Agnes' arm. She was old and frail, and he was worried about the effect this would have on her. "You don't need to worry about breaking any agreement. They are both deceased. You're in no violation of your agreement, and you are under no suspicion. We're going to make sure you get all the protection you need going forward, okay?"

Agnes blotted her eyes with her handkerchief and nodded in understanding. "I never knew she was capable of anything like this. She was such a wonderful woman. Suppressed and controlled, but she wouldn't kill her husband or herself. I don't understand it."

"I know this must be very confusing for you, but we have sufficient evidence that proves this was a murder-suicide. I think it's fair to suggest that both Mr. and Mrs. Alonso had their secrets. Some we may never know."

They continued to talk in the kitchen as the forensics teams got to work. The media outside was already going crazy to catch the slightest bit of information on the wind. The forensics team had found that whatever project Arlo was working on had been taken by Kate, most likely after his death, and reworked in some sinister sort of way. His papers were found scattered around her dead body, smudged and spoiled with blood, and scribbled on in blue crayon. Some of what she wrote was nothing but rambling, while certain words were clear. The thing that had caught the investigators' eyes was a date that appeared to have been written so viciously, it had torn through the page.

"It's something, something ... thirty? Is that a combination? Or a date or something?"

Another forensics officer was glancing over the papers beside the woman who just spoke. "If it's a date, we only know the year, not the day or month." He went through the pages with his gloved hands, a look of terror in his eyes. "This is ... beyond anything I have ever seen in my whole career. End of the world? Ghosts? Jesus reincarnated? Blind men? I don't even know where to start. The word 'crazy' doesn't even come close."

The other officer shook her head as she looked over her colleague's shoulder. "You'd think with all the fame and money, they would have had the most easy, perfect lives."

"Well, sometimes genius is crazy, and money is power."

"I guess you're right."

It took them hours to sift through all the evidence. Everything was covered in blood, and there were so many single pages and origami birds to bag. It was a busy Monday morning, to say the least.

The Constable was outside the black gates of the Alonsos' mansion, standing right in front of the giant 'A' that adorned it and answering the press' many questions. "At this time, I cannot share with you any details, as this is an ongoing case. I can, however, inform you all that today, at 11:27 a.m. Arlo Alonso and his wife, Katherine Alonso, were found dead at the scene. We are currently treating this case as a murder-suicide, and hopefully we will have more information soon.

Thank you."

The Constable quickly moved from his spot as the cameras clicked repetitively and the reporters continued to push microphones into his face for answers. There was no respect anymore. No privacy. As he got into the car, he sighed. The two officers at the front looked back at him.

"Are you okay, sir?"

He nodded and began to loosen his tie. It had been a terrible day, and it was nowhere near being over. He took his phone from his pocket to see he had received two notifications that needed his attention. He sighed, knowing it couldn't be good, and he was more than right.

The first stated:

"Steven Hendrix, more commonly known as 'Barty the Behemoth,' front man and lead singer of Burn the Blazers, has been in a terrible, fatal accident. While the singer was preparing for his grand show in London tonight, it appears some kind of stage failure cost Hendrix his life. Hendrix had received many threats in the last few months regarding his controversial album release, and the police are currently treating the case as suspicious."

The Constable rubbed his tired eyes and looked outside his window briefly. The blur of darkened trees rushed past as they drove, and every so often, glimpses of the pink sky pierced through the haze. He sighed once more and dared to read the second message.

This one stated:

"Michael Gray, renowned actor most famous for his role as the blind man, James, in the hit film *Eyes Without Reason,* has died. While working on his newest film this morning, Gray became violent toward his co-workers and claimed he had become blind. During the struggle, Gray received life-threatening injuries. He died during transport to the nearest hospital. The facts of the case remain a mystery, but police are currently focusing on the mental state of Michael Gray at the time of the attack."

The world was going crazy, the Constable was sure of it. People were changing, the world was changing, and fame had lost its security. It no longer guaranteed anyone's safety, nor did it excuse them for the sins they committed. Even the ones closest to them were becoming accessories to their madness.

A woman appeared next to him, draped in black attire that matched her sleek hair and wearing red high heels that matched the colour of her lips. She extended a hand expectingly to receive the package of evidence sitting in the Constable's lap.

Her devilish smile played on her lips as she removed the papers from the bag, expecting to find the date she had been seeking for eternity: the day when all hell would break loose and the cycle would finally break. But all she found was a partial date that had been smudged by none other than Kate Alonso herself, destroying the crucial information she needed. The rest of the pages were all stained and ruined beyond repair from her fight with Kate, the fight that had reduced it all – every ounce of work and effort – to nothing. *Nothing.* Her eyes flashed flame red as she threw the papers to the floor, and a flurry of pages flew around inside the car as she screamed. By the time the pages floated down to the floor, she was gone.

A smile grew on the Constable's face. If one thing was certain to him in that moment, as the Devil left his presence and the afternoon glow illuminated the back of the car, humanity would survive another day. Thanks to a man who was eager to heal the world of trauma that he himself had suffered, wanting people to believe in a greater force. Thanks to another man who wanted the world to see what it was so blind to in everyday life, a truth that could only be seen through blind faith. And thanks to a woman who had suffered and battled to fight for people she no longer felt loved by, who loved – unconditionally – a humanity to which she didn't even belong. The people of the world would wake up tomorrow like any other day, without a care in the world – to make mistakes, to sin and to spend the rest of their lives making up for it. To do wrong and be human.

All thanks to an asylum.

An asylum of apostles.

Dying is an unexplainable thing. To some, that moment is fuelled with panic and fear. To others it is a moment of bliss and escape. I never considered how I would die or where I would end up afterwards. Maybe I thought death was as meaningless as the life I once had, and it would just consist of nothingness. But I was wrong. About *everything,* for that matter. The world didn't end, and neither did our journey. All three of us sat on the front steps of the Lodge, holding hands as we did before we died. We were waiting. Waiting to be taken away from the place we had been dumped. A limbo between life and death.

As a car approached us, we all stood up, eager to meet

the person we had been so desperate to see. The car was black and unmarked, and two police officers were seated at the front. It stopped and out stepped a man dressed in a suit, his white hair flowing like candyfloss in the evening breeze. At first, his face was stern, and a worry set into my stomach on whom he was, as I was still traumatised from the journey we had just concluded. His face glowed with a warm smile as he held his arms out lovingly.

"My children. You have done well."

I did not see him walk towards us. In fact, I wasn't sure how he managed to move to us as effortlessly as he did. The air smelt of sweet fragrant flowers, and I couldn't tell you if it was from the Lodge gardens or the man who stood in front of us. The day had been cold, but suddenly a warmth filled us all with comfort. It was when Barty began to cry, we knew exactly who had come to collect us.

I went to speak, and He stopped me.

"There is no need to question why, Kate. You had a choice, and you chose to sacrifice yourself for us all. That is all that matters."

I still questioned if I was worthy, and I think we all did in some way. Did we really deserve a place upstairs? But I chose not to argue. The fight had been long, and I was tired. Tired enough to just stop. But I had to know one thing before we left.

"What is this place?"

Michael and Barty were already moving towards the car when I asked the question. The Constable looked at me with a smile. He allowed the others to get into the car as He walked closer to me, holding out an arm.

"Allow me."

As I held on to His arm, a light rushed through my veins and empowered my soul. I had never felt safer in my whole life than I did now, and I had the sudden urge to burst into tears. He gently raised His free hand to wipe the water from my face with His thumb.

"Don't cry, child. There is nothing left to fear."

I nodded in acceptance and began walking with Him slowly through the garden of the Lodge, watching the flowers sway in the sunset.

"This place was built by my own hands. It is not heaven, and it is not hell. It was to be a safe haven for those who had not yet found their way."

"So, it is true? We died?"

He continued to walk with a look of sympathy on His face, an understanding of how hard the transition between life and death was for us. "I am afraid so, and before your intended time, may I add. I tried my best to collect you all, but I was too late. My fallen child had already taken you and corrupted this place in order to fulfil a prophecy that should never have been written." He sighed deeply between His explanations. "You see, Kate, the balance between good and evil is not so simple. There is no straightforward solution, and neither is there a clear path. I do believe, however, that humanity deserves a chance to learn how to balance itself. Without divine intervention. In a war between angels and demons, you always seem to become the pawns, and that is my fault. It is something I never intended to happen. But despite it all, you three are living proof that humanity deserves a chance. Especially you, Kate."

"Did you know what choice I would make? I was the key to the end of the world, and I-"

"You weren't sure if you had destroyed it or not. I know." He laughed gently and stopped walking to face me. "You had a choice. One to make on behalf of them all. Even though you weren't sure what you were, or what you had become, you still made the right one. But in answer to your question, as all-knowing as I am, no. I did not know what you would choose. But I am proud of the choice you made."

I looked back at the Lodge, then at the car that waited for me. I knew it was time to go and put this all behind us.

"They are waiting for you. It is time for you to rest, Kate. It is your time to be free."

I liked the sound of that. The truth was, I was ready. I was ready to rest. I just needed one thing before I could. I asked God for something I never thought I would.

"What about Arlo?"

He beamed at me like a proud father and replied.

"He is waiting for you."

And with that, I walked my last steps to the car, down the gravelled road of the Lodge, never looking back at the place that had confined me. I got into the back to find Barty and Michael happy to see me, as if they had questioned whether I was going with them. In unison, they asked me a simple question.

"Are you ready?"

I looked down at the floor, bracing myself for this last trip, when I saw a singular origami bird folded from a Bible page. It was mine. I held it between my fingers, turning it over to see the word "Genesis" printed on it. This was a new beginning for us all. The first chapter of a new book. Barty held out his hand to take the bird, his palm marked from his iconic death. Bearing the mark of Christ.

I looked back up at both Barty and Michael, and replied. "I'm ready."

Acknowledgements

They say it takes a village. Well, this time it took my own personal asylum! I would like to thank all the *crazy* people who believed in me from the offset. I never thought I would ever get to the point of being confident enough to write a whole book, no matter how small, and as I am writing this now, I am 250 pages deep into my next adventure. So, a big thank you to everyone who has supported me throughout this journey and whoever has picked this book up to read! I would like to personally thank my brother, KK, for being one of my biggest inspirations in everything I do, with his own unique ideas and invaluable input. Of course, another big thank you to both of my parents who have always supported me and the crazy decisions I make. Another personal thank you goes to Daniel, the bestie, who is always ready to read and rummage through my rough ramblings and help turn them into something that resembles prose, even when my ideas are beyond insane. Finally, a massive thank you to my editor, Mary, for turning my book into something wonderful (and professional).

About the Author

Monique Müge is an accomplished illustrator, self-confessed nerd and avid crochet-aholic. She has a collection of invisible medical conditions, such as Hypermobile Ehlers-Danlos Syndrome and Fibromyalgia. Her experiences living with these conditions fuel her desire to include disability awareness in her work, and she refuses to let her health rule her life.

After helping to save her favourite TV show, *Daredevil*, Monique rediscovered her passion and love for the creative arts. She graduated with a MA in Children's Book Illustration and Graphic Novels in 2023, after which she started to regularly write.

She continues to work on other projects, updates of which can be found across all of her socials.

Instagram: @moniquemuge
Email: moniquemuge@gmail.com

Printed in Great Britain
by Amazon

43871010R00078